THE
UTOPIA
CHRONICLES

T0051114

Also by Matthew Mather

Atopia Series

The Atopia Chronicles

The Dystopia Chronicles

Nomad Series

Nomad

Sanctuary

Stand-Alone Novels

CyberStorm

Darknet

THE UTOPIA CHRONICLES

MATTHEW
MATHER

47NORTH

This is a work of fiction. Names, characters, organizations, places, events, and incidents are either products of the author's imagination or are used fictitiously. Any resemblance to actual persons, living or dead, or actual events is purely coincidental.

Published by 47North, Seattle

www.apub.com

Amazon, the Amazon logo, and 47North are trademarks of Amazon.com, Inc., or its affiliates.

ISBN-13: 9781477848371
ISBN-10: 1477848371

Cover design by Jason Blackburn
Cover illustrated by Paul Youll

Printed in the United States of America

For Leila and Kenya

Preface

I finished writing *The Utopia Chronicles* on the five hundredth anniversary of the first publishing of the original *Utopia* by the English statesman and philosopher Thomas More. *Utopia*, in turn, was inspired by Plato's *Republic*, published about 380 BC, and my Atopia series is intended to be both an homage and a modern update on the themes and visions of these works.

If the description of an ideal city-state of the future, located on an island off the coast of the New World, sounds familiar to readers of my series, that's because I borrowed this same plot device from the original *Utopia*. More's narrative work describes a world without hardship, and in fact, the common usage of the word "utopia" derives from More's work (originally published in Latin). In creating my Atopia series, I tried to envision what today's generation might imagine an ultimate utopia to embody: a place where everyone is free to do whatever they please, wherever they want, and in unlimited excess.

Of course, there is always a darker side to paradise, and that is much of the topic of the rest of the series, but in *The Utopia Chronicles*, I turn the finale inward to explore the conundrums of existence and the possible ultimate nature of reality in our churning technological future.

Matthew Mather
October 11, 2016

Introduction

This is the third and final book of the Atopia Chronicles series. For readers who would like a synopsis of the events, places, and characters in the first two books, the following pages summarize *The Atopia Chronicles* and *The Dystopia Chronicles*. You can, of course, skip this and get straight into *The Utopia Chronicles*.

THE ATOPIA CHRONICLES

The first book is told through a series of five stories that reveal the world one step at a time, then a final, longer story that ties them all together. All the stories start at the same moment.

Prologue

Dr. Patricia Killiam, lead researcher for Cognix Corporation, discovers an unusual signal in the data from the Pacific Ocean Neutrino Detector (POND). Dr. Killiam and her staff are located on Atopia, a vast floating city-state in the Pacific, just off the coast of California. Her staff believes that the signal comes from the deep reaches of interstellar space, from an alien civilization. The message seems to be some kind of warning, directed at Atopia. Dr. Killiam warns her staff not to tell anyone about the signal.

Blue Skies

Olympia Onassis is an advertising executive living in the bustling metropolis of late-twenty-first-century New York City. She is in charge of a program to bring Dr. Killiam's new virtual reality product, pssi—the poly-synthetic sensory interface—into the market. It is by far the largest marketing program of all time, with an advertising launch budget of billions of dollars.

The stress is enormous, and Olympia suffers from panic disorder. Her doctor recommends a synthetic reality system that can block out advertising, a beta test of the new product that she is in charge of launching publicly in a few months. She agrees, installing the pssi by swallowing a glass of water containing trillions of smarticles that suffuse into her nervous system. When she gets home, she is introduced to her proxxi—a personal digital assistant that appears in augmented reality. It looks exactly like Olympia and is the digital control and interface to her new synthetic reality.

Her new system can erase not just advertisements but anything that is bothering her: garbage from the street, graffiti from walls, homeless people. One morning she awakes and decides to go for a run. Halfway to Central Park, she notices that nobody else is around. No cars. No people. The city is deathly silent, devoid of people, everywhere she searches.

Olympia takes an automated passenger transport to other cities around the world—but it is the same everywhere. Nobody. She is the last person left on the version of Earth she has become stuck in.

Childplay

Rick Strong is the new Commander of the Atopian Defense Force (ADF), a former US Marine who fought in the first Weather Wars. He came to Atopia with his wife, Cindy, a second chance for them after Rick's combat PTSD and her depressive episodes. Cindy wants to have a child, but Rick isn't ready. He has an idea: to try proxxids, virtual reality children, simulations using the real DNA of the parents. Reluctantly Cindy agrees, and a day later, little Ricky appears in the new virtual nursery room in their apartment.

Cindy begins to experiment more with the synthetic reality system, adding new rooms to their house, then creating whole new homes in augmented reality, taking the family on trips around the world, all without leaving the confines of Atopia. How fast the kids grow up: after just a month, little Ricky is already four years old. Rick decides they're ready to have a real child, but now Cindy wants to try a few new proxxids first.

Rick gets angry. He's under stress. Atopia faces daily cyberattacks, believed to be from Terra Nova, a competing offshore colony based in the Atlantic Ocean, just off Africa's west coast. Massive hurricanes appear in both the Pacific and Atlantic Ocean basins, a sequence of four storms behaving very strangely. Rick has to move Atopia, a floating island near the coast of America.

Cindy falls into another depression and commits "reality suicide," a mental isolation where the pssi user cuts off all connections to reality. Rick rushes to the hospital, where he finds his wife in what appears to be a coma. Further investigation reveals that the proxxids had aged at horrific speeds. Cindy spent their last days with them, six proxxid children who died in a matter of months. Now she hides in a self-imposed prison, replaying memories where nobody can reach her.

Timedrops

A man hides inside an autonomous drone aircraft at the edge of the atmosphere, trying to escape Atopia using the slingshot weapons test as a diversion—but he miscalculates. The weapon fires and lights the atmosphere into a searing wall of flame that consumes the drone and kills the man.

Vince Indigo is the famous trillionaire founder of Phuture News, a twenty-four-hour news network that reports on the news of the future. Combined with pssi, Phuture News allows people on Atopia not just to read about possible future events but to actually experience them.

Vince was the man in the drone, but the event didn't really happen—at least not in the timeline where Vince still lives. A phuture is just a possible future based on the "nearly infinite multiverse" model of physics. The drone event was just one of hundreds of ways Vince may die in the next few days.

As the owner of the Phuture News Network, Vince has access to the most advanced future predictions on the planet, and he fights off hundreds of future death threats every day. Vince ultimately finds comfort only by visiting a monastery in Lhasa, among Buddhist statues with multiple arms and heads, living in timeless worlds.

Brothers Blind

Robert Baxter is one of the first generation of pssi-kids, born on Atopia twenty years ago, the first humans to live their whole lives with access to unlimited virtual reality. Bob dropped out of the Atopian pssi-kid academy as a teenager and has earned his living hosting his own dimstim. Other people jack into his sensory channels to experience physically what it's like to be one of the world's greatest surfers. He never turns it off, much to the annoyance of a parade of girlfriends.

Though his father is the head of public relations for Atopia, Bob has dropped off into a self-indulgent world of drug abuse and video games, amplified in endless virtual worlds. He and his best friend, Sid, take psychoactive substances and play in gameworlds, hunting down Genghis Khan on the steppes of Asia or stealing cars in 1980s Los Angeles.

Bob's drug use spirals out of control, even as the hurricanes threaten Atopia. An evacuation is ordered, and Bob's brother, Martin, discovers that his name isn't on the evacuation manifest. Bob tells Martin why he never sees his proxxi. Martin actually died four years before, a suicide.

His family used the Atopian virtual reality system to resurrect Martin's proxxi and make it think it was their son. Martin breaks down into tears.

Neverywhere

William McIntyre is one of Sid and Bob's best friends. He attended the pssi-kid academy, but he wasn't born on Atopia. He was brought there when he was seven years old, from the Commune, a massive compound in the foothills of the Montana Rockies.

Nancy Killiam is Willy's childhood friend and the love of Bob's life, although they've been estranged since Bob sank himself into drugs. Nancy is also the inventor of a distributed-consciousness technology being offered to the public through her newly formed company, Infinixx. The launch event is to be held in Atopia's main ballroom, culminating in the throwing of a physical switch that routes power into the main processing core, linking individual systems in India, China, and more.

When the time comes, Nancy asks her aunt, Patricia Killiam, to do the honors—but Patricia informs her that she is only there in her virtual presence. Nancy quickly asks everyone on the stage with her, but though the ballroom is packed with people, nobody is there in person. Everyone sent their virtual avatars, including Nancy herself. The world media laughs as billions of people watch a switch that nobody can throw. The media disaster throws Atopian stocks into turmoil.

Soon after, Willy approaches Bob with a strange realization—someone stole his physical body away from Atopia, but he doesn't seem to mind. He stops obsessing over money and focuses on his relationship with his girlfriend. Maybe on Atopia, a physical body isn't really necessary. Maybe his proxxi, Wally, stole his body as a way of trying to help him understand this.

Genesis and Janus

Jimmy Scadden is Bob's adopted brother. His mother was distantly related to Patricia Killiam, but his parents mysteriously left Atopia when Jimmy was barely a teenager. He didn't have an easy time growing up: his mother trapped him in claustrophobic virtual worlds when he was a child, before he had full control over his own pssi system. Sometimes she used these simulated worlds to torture him, directly accessing his pain systems in a way that left no marks but was excruciating.

At a Cognix Corporation Board meeting, Patricia brings up a strange string of disappearances—people whose minds have disappeared into virtual worlds and who either can't find their way back out or refuse to. Dozens and perhaps hundreds of people have disappeared. Troubled, she decides to open up a private virtual world into her past. She is over a hundred years old, once a student of Alan Turing in the years just before he took his own life in Cambridge, England. At the time, Turing had just proposed his own famous test for determining sentience: if a black box came down out of the sky and we talked with whatever was inside, if we couldn't tell if it was a person or not, then by definition it was an intelligent being inside, whether human, artificial, or otherwise.

At the time, Patricia had put forward her own thesis. By the same token, she hypothesized that if a conscious observer couldn't distinguish between a simulated reality and the real world, then didn't the simulated reality meet the criteria for being as "real" as the real world? Did perception actually create reality? The question has haunted Patricia for a hundred years, and now, with stress mounting, Patricia suffers a kind of stroke and is incapacitated. Her doctors reveal that she doesn't have long to live.

Martial law and a state of emergency are declared as storms threaten to crush Atopia against the coast of America. Control of all systems is taken from Patricia—but strangely, almost none of the half-million inhabitants want to leave, even in the face of imminent death. Jimmy suggests a last-ditch plan to save Atopia by using the slingshot weapons to burn a hole through the churning hurricanes. The Board gives Jimmy control of all Atopia's systems to try to make it happen. Patricia is the only abstainer.

Bob wants to find out what is going on, so he smuggles himself, Nancy, Sid, and Vince down to the computing core of Atopia, five hundred feet below the waterline. They plug directly in and almost immediately see the truth that has been hiding in front of them: pssi is intensely addictive, and Patricia is going to hook the world on virtual crack cocaine—and more, she is trying to kill Vince.

Bob confronts Patricia, and she admits that it's all true. For more than fifty years, she has been perfecting the futuring technology with Vince, always with the same end result: total apocalypse driven by mankind's insatiable appetite for physical luxury. The only way forward was to move people into a world of virtual consumption, effectively putting the human race to sleep for a generation while the planet healed itself—but at the cost of turning humanity into a collective junky.

Hurricanes begin to blast the surface of Atopia, ripping it apart—but Jimmy decides not to light up the slingshots. Patricia fights for control against him, but he disables her and then reveals why.

There were never any storms.

It's too late for Patricia, though. She's about to die, but she reveals that Jimmy Scadden is a dangerous sociopath who has wormed his way into control of Atopia, stealing people's minds, trapping and torturing them in virtual worlds they can't escape. In a last act of desperation, she leaves a message for Bob and his friends. Leave Atopia, she tells them, and find William McIntyre's body. It holds the key.

THE DYSTOPIA CHRONICLES

Commander Stockard is captain of the deep space Comet Catcher mission, tasked with ferrying comet Wormwood into Earth's orbit. The mission has been going smoothly for two months, but he suddenly finds himself hallucinating, staring at his dead mother floating inside the main cabin. Just moments before, the entire night side of Earth winked on and off and on again. What is going on?

Two months before, Nancy Killiam smuggled herself into a secret virtual meeting in which Jimmy Scadden was recruiting his own private cyber army. She's trying to figure out what Jimmy is up to and where Bob, Sid, and Vince took off to when they left Atopia.

Her friends are in Montana but have gone off-grid, trying to get inside the Commune. High in the sky over Montana, they see the comet Wormwood appear—and Bob has visions of living with green skin in a strange world with green creatures. The Commune won't let Bob in, but they will let Vince in. He goes inside and finds out that it's run by the Reverend McIntyre, Willy's grandfather, and that Willy—or at least Willy's body—had been there just a week before. The Reverend says that the Apocalypse is upon them and that Willy had been researching ancient texts there.

Bob and Sid go to New York, where more than half the people have already plugged into the Atopian pssi technology. Billboards are filled with images of Jimmy Scadden. A bomb goes off, and Sid is kidnapped, but Bob manages to escape into a passenger cannon that sails on a trajectory high over the Atlantic toward Terra Nova. Vince had been on his way to New York to meet them, but he was intercepted by the FBI, arrested, and redirected to Cuba.

Bob's pod is diverted halfway over the Atlantic, and he realizes he's in trouble, so he contacts Nancy and tells her everything he knows about Jimmy. He wakes up in a dusty, primitive jail cell in the middle of the Sahara desert, caught by bounty hunters, he assumes. After a fight, he escapes into the desert with a mysterious man who calls himself the priest and who inundates Bob with talk of the religious and philosophical, about paths to the cessation of suffering.

Sid finds himself deep in the bowels of New York. He tracks Willy's body through other cities around the world before it disappears in

Southeast Asia. He investigates the tunnels it passed through and finds clumps of strange crystals there.

Vince's transport is attacked again and this time crashes into swamps around New Orleans. He contacts the gangster Mikhail Butorin, who admits that he smuggled Willy's body out of Atopia and that it was carrying secret information about who was controlling Jimmy, but he lost track of where Willy's body went. Butorin suggests that Jimmy has been infected with an ancient evil that the gangster met a hundred years before, when he was one of the team that dug up the Nag Hammadi texts in Egypt. He shows Vince an ancient scroll, translated as "Book of Pobeptoc," with the line "Wal lie body is where the flesh eaters live."

Meanwhile, Jimmy has convinced Allied Command—made up of America and India together with Atopia and others—that it was Terra Nova that attacked them. He gets agreement for the Allies to launch a massive attack. With the priest's help, Bob crosses northern Africa out of Allied territory. He contacts Terra Nova, and Tyrel—their leader—agrees to retrieve him and immediately asks for the data cube that Patricia left him. Bob is suspicious and holds back. The world media discovers that Bob has made his way into Terra Nova, and this becomes proof of the massive conspiracy theories already brewing.

Vince and Sid guess that Willy's body is in Papua New Guinea, with the Yupno tribe. They find Willy's body there, inhabited by his proxxi, who admits that it stole the body to protect Willy. Tyrel confirms the existence, underneath human cities, of the dark quasi-crystals, an ancient evil that has destroyed the Earth before, and that the apocalypse Patricia foresaw is true—Jimmy is the White Horseman foretold in the Apocalypse, controlled by the Great Destroyer.

Bob smuggles his physical body back to Atopia and surprises Jimmy with the information that Jimmy has been infected by something. Nancy had been trying to displace him, but he traps her and threatens to kill her. Bob unleashes a massive cyberattack inside of Atopia. Jimmy counters it, and Bob comes up with a desperate plan to insert himself directly into the Atopian computing core. This time he dives five hundred feet into the frigid depths outside the Atopian hull using his superhuman swimming skills, and the effort all but kills him. Bob's physical body dies as he inserts his control memories into the Atopian core.

Allied forces have begun their attack on Terra Nova. Sid decodes what's inside of Willy's data, and this unpacks the POND data. Sid is stupefied to find memory streams of Bob, but a different Bob living thousands of different lives on alien worlds. It doesn't make any sense.

Bob's digital mind blossoms into awareness inside of the Atopia networks, allowing him control over all the Atopian system, including access to both Allied and Terra Novan weapons platforms. Despite stopping Jimmy, he is horrified to find Nancy's dead body on the surface of Atopia. He was too late.

Parts of Bob's and Jimmy's minds begin to release all the people Jimmy had trapped and tortured. Olympia Onassis wakes to people all around her. Cindy Strong wakes and tearfully embraces her husband. Thousands of disappeared people awake back into the world.

Bob's mind fragments, and his emotions flare into anger, self-loathing, and hatred. He sees the terrible weapon that the Great Destroyer has begun to unleash. He realizes that not all the people trapped in the mysterious dark crystals are people whom Jimmy stole but that the crystals have existed since before humans—and contain a record of every human. He wakes them, and each human from all time blossoms back to life in connected virtual worlds.

But only for an instant. The supercollider ignites, ripping a hole in the fabric of space and triggering a quantum meta-stability event. In the blink of an eye, Earth is destroyed, and a wave of lower-energy-state vacuum spreads out at the speed of light, consuming everything in its path. Bob's mind decodes some of the memories—some of his memories—and collates them into a burst of neutrinos that carries forth on the wave front.

This universe is gone—but another has begun.

Part I

1

"What does it mean?" The Engineer paused before she answered her own question: "It means the end, and it means the beginning."

"Of what?" Vollix Hardadiss's collective affected surprised confusion.

Tiny flickers, at first soothingly random, but then all the same: one after another, one after the next—all the same. It would have meant nothing, just an accumulation of chance, if the Engineer could have ignored the sensation of dread as black as a starless sky. No theorems, no more explanations, thought the Engineer in her most private of inner sanctuaries. Now it had become a matter of faith, and that wasn't something she could explain to the Vollix. Not in the time they had left.

The Engineer smiled and lied to Vollix Hardadiss: "It means the end of our Project." And this was the truth, but not in the way the Hardadiss would understand it.

"Of course." A grin, something between ingratiating and threatening, spread across the Vollix splinters' emotive networks. This collective didn't believe the Engineer, but then it was also afraid of her. "When can we expect the handover?" it asked, still maintaining a cloak of formality that barely hid the angular lines of threat beneath.

"As soon as we have carried out the first tests."

"And what is the purpose?"

"I've already explained—"

"Explain again." This Hardadiss collective opened its mindspace, invitingly but forcefully, tired of the bride refusing to come to its bedchamber.

"If you cannot understand, then I have no more time to indulge you." The Engineer snapped the connection shut.

The Hardadiss squirmed and opened an outdated radio channel. "We will remind you—"

"*We* need no reminding."

Deals had been made and compromises brokered for the Engineer to amass this vast trove of resources, the sum total of almost everything the Umebak had been building steadily toward for millennia. It came down to this, this one moment, and the Engineer needed to concentrate her many minds to the task at hand.

"The first distortion will reach the homeworld?" Vollix Hardadiss persisted, refusing to be dismissed.

"That is the goal."

"And then?"

"Then many more. But first we reach Sood."

The homeworld was a place the Engineer had almost forgotten. Her physical—biological—body had long since perished, but her soul remained as an ephemeral dance of energy. The Umebak race had released its shackles one by one: at first the individual and then the biological. One by one, the old animal desires had almost been extinguished, yet the desire for power remained. Would always remain, the Engineer now wearily understood. The desire for power over the universe itself.

In the end, power for its own sake.

In its most literal sense, the Project embodied that eternal desire. The physicality of it stretched into the distance below her virtual viewpoint, a dark mass of millions of photonic arrays. Each single array was vaster in area than the gas giant planets that orbited beyond the Project's sphere encompassing this hot blue star, its radiant energy now almost blotted out. They were harvesting the star's energy—*all* of it.

The clans were on the brink of war. Once again. This time, the Engineer wasn't sure she could pull them back from the edge, but it didn't matter anymore. She was tired. Beyond tired. How many years now? Five hundred and sixteen, but these were years measured as rotations of a planet around another star now distant in both space and time. Time itself seemed a quaint conception. To her reconstructed conscious streams of thought, a nanosecond could be stretched into an eternity, and an eternity could fit into the blink of an eye. Time was an emergent phenomenon of the underlying connectedness of everything in this universe, the Engineer now understood, but only to observers *within* this universe; to observers without, it was absent, had no meaning, no direction, no substance.

She was trapped within.

The Engineer focused on a stream of consciousness monitoring the qubits. One and then the next, she opened the circuits to discover the spin of each, and they were all coming up the same. Each qubit was entangled with its pair at creation, unobserved, and sent off into space on tiny spacecraft, their cargo smaller than a microbe, their gossamer wings capturing the focused energy of each photonic array, sending them speeding away into the ether surrounding this blue star. This part of the Project she had explained as a monitoring of local conditions, an experiment to verify that the laws of nature were unbending. For a hundred years, the Engineer had been sending out tiny explorers, each accelerating to within a whisker of the speed of light, the absolute speed limit—but light wasn't really the speed limit. Light just happened to travel at the speed of causality, the fastest speed at which one thing could affect another, measured in time or in space—and massless photons bumped up against the causal limit.

No useful information could surpass this speed limit.

And yet the Engineer suspected she had somehow.

The fixed spin of each quantum-entangled qubit that the Engineer observed matched the spin of another dispatched on one of the tiny spaceships. It was an effect that, at first blush, seemed to crush the speed of causality, but it didn't, because although it gave her instantaneous information about something arbitrarily far away, it was random. Up or down. She shouldn't have been able to predict the outcome, and for the first few thousand, the results were soothingly random. Then began the streak. Up. Up. And up again. Parts of the sphere still remained random, but a wave front rushed toward her. Rushed toward her at the speed of causality.

Only hours remained.

She'd hidden the impending destruction from the Council, from the Galagat, from the Hardadiss.

The Engineer hadn't cut this final communication channel. It was too risky, but she needed to focus. "Vollix, if you will allow me?" The time had come to disconnect the last of the arrays from their outward beaming of energy into the swarm and redirect the energy of this star inward. "I must excuse myself." The Engineer politely but firmly closed the last of her connections to the clans' systems.

The energy of the star pulsed through her, her extrasensory networks caressing it, channeling it into the purpose-built collector fabricated from the remnants of this star system's asteroid belts. Invisible lines of energy bent around the sphere of the Project, funneling and amplifying into the true and final aim, a sheath of negative energy that would punch a hole through the very fabric of space itself.

A wormhole.

To answer the age-old question that had plagued the Umebak race: Why is nobody else out there?

In the five-hundred-plus years that the Umebak had been a spacefaring civilization, their informational network had grown to a sphere a hundred light-years across, centered on the homeworld of Sood. Their tiny ships, propelled on beams of energy, had visited almost all the ten thousand stars within this expanding sphere of influence. Nearly five hundred were stars that matched the spectral type of their own sun.

Hundreds of billions of stars in their galaxy, a hundred billion galaxies in the visible extent of the universe. Around almost each and every star, a collection of planets. Over a quarter of stars had planets within the habitable zone, where liquid water and energy collected in enough abundance to enable life to self-organize.

And it did.

The Umebak found life in almost every nook and cranny they explored. Hundreds of worlds teeming with it, washed from star system to star system, microscopic fragments of life coughed into space on waves of cataclysmic collisions, frozen in the vacuum, and distributed on the currents of stellar winds. Evolutionary pressures forced a collective intelligence into the creatures, but none surpassed the threshold for technical civilization.

Their own homeworld was the only place in the universe the Umebak knew, for certain, that a space-faring civilization had evolved. In that five hundred years, though they had listened, they had heard nothing from the stars. Was it possible that their civilization was a fluke? The only one that existed? That had *ever* existed? The odds were astronomically against it. About one in ten billion trillion that they were alone in their own galaxy, based on their own understanding of the spread of life between stars and the structure of the universe around them.

And in the observable universe, the odds stretched to one in a billion trillion trillion.

Odds beyond possible.

So something else was going on. Something that made the clans nervous.

What was out there? Did it threaten the Umebak? How?

To answer the question required a technology that would allow the Umebak to travel farther and faster than the speed limit of causality.

They would have to open holes in space, which required the focused energy of ten times their own sun's. Thus the Project was born, to harness the power of this massive blue star, to bend space and time to their will. All to answer the question.

In that same five hundred years, the Umebak hadn't just been listening. In that time, the ugly burn for power had destroyed half the worlds they had inhabited. The Umebak civilization itself had narrowly missed its own extinction a dozen times. If other civilizations were anything like them, the Engineer had more than an inkling of why nobody else might have been out there. It was only through the Engineer's sheer force of will that she had pulled the clans back from the edge each time in that five hundred years, each return to grace more tenuous than the last.

Her hold over them was based on fear. Fear of her power. Of her mysterious technical abilities.

That power surged through the Engineer's extrasensory networks, and she focused her mind on the shimmering halo of negative energy, her probes poised to enter—but a part of her mind remained fixed, looking out at the steel pinpricks of stars against the oil slick of sky. Looking into the sky was the same as looking back in time. The light from the stars took hundreds, even millions and tens of millions of years, to reach here. The sky looked the same. Solid. Unchanging.

But she knew different.

2

Robert Baxter squinted in the bright morning sunshine, shielded his eyes with his right hand to get a better look at the shimmering ocean's surface. He pulled forward on his surfboard, balanced it beneath himself as he sat waist-deep in the bobbing swells. Scanning the horizon once again, he closed his eyes and concentrated on his water sense, felt the rise of the water's surface, the eddy currents pulling at his feet, the tiny creatures swirling below in the depths. His senses pushed outward, spinning away from his physical body, feeling the water now as a layer of his skin, each riffle of the ocean's surface a caress along his back and arms. Farther and farther, his mind's eye sped across the ocean's surface as he felt out each coming swell, evaluated its shape and texture—and then he found the one.

A tiny splinter—a subset of his mind's cognitive function—replicated itself and set off to backtrack in time through the global wikiworld to research the development of this wave of interest. He wanted to know everything about it. The first reliable data on the formation of this wave set showed it had developed seventeen hours ago in an arctic hurricane still raging across the Bering Sea four thousand miles away. The wave packet had gained energy as it swept past the Aleutian chain of islands, encouraged by southerly winds, and combined with another chop of waves off Hawaii. A distant storm system coming across the Pacific from the

Philippines had provided the final push, and this wave had met another wave set reflected from the coast of America.

Robert published all this information into his social cloud for his fans.

"Nice wave," said Gloria Davis from Nashville, stim-switching her senses into Robert's for the impending surf ride. Together with sixty-eight other followers, she led a modeling assessment that plotted the course of the wave around the northern rim. It would top out at twenty-one feet. The best of the day. "I'm in too!" clamored hundreds more followers as the Phuture News posting gained strength and cleared new altitude in Robert's social cloud.

One by one, Robert felt them click into him, each of his fans substituting his senses for theirs—they heard what he heard, they felt what he felt, and they saw what he saw. To start the show, he glanced across the waves, past the beaches and harbor breakwater inlets, at the glittering spires of the Atopian seastead. Glass towers pierced a thousand feet into clear blue sky. His surfboard sat submerged at the edge of the genetically engineered kelp forests, their gas-bladder holdfasts an army of green goblins that spread across the ocean's surface to his back.

"Can you do a back hang?" asked Bill Ruzedsky from Des Moines.

"I want a rocket water board," countered Leslie Finegold from New York.

"Everyone in the back," Robert subtexted to his horde of dimstim followers. He shut down the conversation streams of his splintered consciousness and focused on the wave. One by one his fans jostled their way into his sensory stream and left his frontal lobes alone. "This is going to be amazing," he broadcast to them all, but really speaking to nobody but himself.

Sliding onto his stomach on the board, he took deep strokes into the water. In a virtual workspace, another splinter calculated and recalculated the optimal path. He was going too slow to reach the best drop-in point, so he pulled harder through the water and summoned a cloud of phytoplankton—always hovering just below—to boil up the water, to help him jet forward across the surface.

Cheating perhaps, but then using Atopian technology for wave riding was always cheating the surfing gods. How many fans had stim-switched into his sensory broadcast so far? Two hundred and twenty-six. Fifty from within Atopia itself, from among the million souls on this seastead floating off the coast of California. Sensory broadcast was still in its infancy in the outside world, but soon that would change. In just weeks Atopian pssi—the poly-synthetic sensory interface technology—would be launched in one of the biggest media campaigns the world had ever seen. Right now he was cheating the gods, but soon everyone would be just like him—like gods themselves—with unlimited access to sensory-perfect virtual reality.

Robert pulled harder into the water.

Still hundreds of yards away, the wave gained mass and shape. It filled his water sense, and his virtual body grew in size, the energy of the swell pushing down against the outer edge of the Atopian sea structure below. Friction dragged the wave's bottom half back while the top surged forward. Finally, it crested, and within fractions of a foot, Robert reached his spot. His hands pressed flat against the surfboard, he rushed down the wave's face, jumped to his feet, and dug backward into the water as the wall thundered over the top, curling into a madly rushing vortex.

"Bob!" someone screamed.

A churlish smile morphed the watery tumult, the image jammed across all of Robert's visual displays. Someone overrode his controls. Bob skipped off the top of the wave—at first tried to ignore the intruder—but then settled into a midwave coast and put his body into his proxxi's control. It could only be one person. The smile resolved into the pale, bushy-black-eyebrowed, spiky-haired face of Bob's best buddy, Sid.

"Are you going to the sensorgy party tonight?" his friend asked.

Bob shifted his body farther back on the board to push them higher on the wave. His proxxi took things a little too carefully, even for a synthetic digital organism that was designed, first and foremost, to protect his physical body. "Of course," Bob replied to Sid.

"Don't forget it's your brother's birthday tomorrow morning," Bob's proxxi, Robert, intervened. At the same time, he eased Bob's physical body farther forward to a safer position on the rushing wave. The wind ripped at his hair.

Bob, feeling somewhat churlish himself, ignored his proxxi. How could he forget it was his brother, Martin's, birthday tomorrow? How stupid did his proxxi think he was? Then again, it was his proxxi's job to defend him. Maybe it wasn't so stupid after all. His mother and father would be crushed if Bob didn't show up *again* this year.

For some people, calling their proxxi by their own full name might have been confusing. But nobody called him Robert. He was known as Bob, to his friends and to his legions of fans. Only his mother called him Robert—and only when she was mad—but she had given him the name, so he reserved the right to her. For him, from anyone else, Robert was a derogatory term, so he reserved the term for his digital alter ego. He could always be mad at himself.

"I'll be there," Bob responded, leaving a yawning pause of fractions of a second before answering Sid and his proxxi, Robert, at the same time. "Can both of you leave me alone?" He sensed his fans getting restless under his skin. They couldn't see this private-channel communication he was having, but they weren't getting to enjoy his usual gymnastics on the wave. Bob snapped closed the comms connection—having plugged the security hole Sid had exploited—took back control of his physical body, and refocused on his ride.

The glittering wave-wall rushed at him. He knelt lower, felt the jittering skip of wavelets rolling up beneath him, and began. Back and forth he cut into the wave, snapped turns off the top, spun around, and let himself slide back. The wave developed into a perfect almond-shaped tube that rolled around the northern edge of the Atopian structure. He had a mile or more left in it, and used every inch to thrill the dimstimmers riding inside.

Even with his cognitive focus centered, the edges of his mind still crackled with ads and infomercials touting the benefits of pssi. He couldn't escape the media blitz. Misdirected advertising. As one of the first children with pssi—the media called them pssi-kids—implanted in their nervous systems from an early age, he'd been a part of the Atopian experiment from the beginning. They couldn't tell virtual worlds from the real thing, the media said. Maybe they were right, and maybe that was the reason Robert liked to stick to his physical body. So he wouldn't get lost in the endless mirror mazes of virtual spaces. There wasn't anything else Robert could possibly learn about Atopian pssi because he wasn't just a user of the technology.

He *was* the technology.

But now he was an unwilling participant.

Once he had been the star pupil of the pssi-kid academy, the pride of Patricia Killiam, founder of Atopia and godmother of synthetic reality and artificial intelligence. All that had come to a crashing end when his brother killed himself—the same brother whose birthday it was tomorrow, the same brother his mother and father refused to recognize had even killed himself. On Atopia, even death had become a mere speed bump on the road to progress.

And now . . .

Now . . .

Bob was what?

Now he was a surfer. A proud miscreant who had joined the thousands of other pssi-kids who had dropped off the edges. With access to unlimited virtual reality from birth, with every need taken care of, with everything they could ever want already given, what did the elders of Atopia expect? Had Patricia expected them all to take their gifts and rise above, to become a race of super-children? Perhaps it had started out like that, when they were young, but Atopia was founded on strict libertarian principles. People were free to do what they wanted, and once the pssi-kids had become teenagers, they had started to do what they wanted—and most of that involved sex and drugs, but on a scale and intensity only possible with Atopian technology.

So while he was an unwilling participant in the grand project, he still used the technology, just like everyone else who had been gifted it. He used pssi to surf like a god. To play unending virtual gameworlds. And to bend his senses. A mixture of synthetic ketamine and organic mushrooms was his and Sid's current favorite cocktail, and later today they'd be meeting up in the virtual world of Humungous Fungus below the Looking Glass to watch the slingshot weapons test together, a huge dance and sensorgy party for the pssi-kids.

Still carving turns into the wave, Bob released his physical body's control to his proxxi again—Robert could handle a few turns—and pulled his viewpoint back to inspect himself. Blond dreadlocks flowed fearlessly in the wind, his eyes as fierce and blue as the sky above, his skin tanned dark. Sinewy muscles roped down his back and his arms. His body twisted, spun backward into the wave, and coasted high toward the frothing peak before snapping a turn off the top and racing back down the face. Only half a mile left on this wave.

The wind whipped his hair. Salt water sprayed and splashed across his body as the wave rolled on. The bright sun shone down. In the back of his mind, thousands of dimstim fans applauded his ride. The wave's tube collapsed behind him and the surge of it subsided, so Bob coasted off the top and sank into the water, offering a flourish of thanks to his followers. He wiped the sting of salt water from his eyes and watched a seagull wheel high in the sky.

Just another day in paradise.

Somewhere in the back of his mind, a tingling dread began. At first, just a tremble, but then an itch and a flash of pain, the crack of a wound opening up. Something was wrong.

"Robert, hey, do you feel that?" Bob flitted into his virtual workspace. Walls of overlaid visual displays monitoring his physical and digital systems glowed bright. He scanned them. No alarms tripped. Nothing was wrong. Robert, his proxxi, stood beside him in the virtual workspace.

"What's wrong?" Robert frowned, inspecting the systems again.

Bob checked and rechecked himself. "I don't know."

Nothing was wrong, not with his body, not with his digital defenses, either.

But there it was.

A growing sense of doom.

He couldn't visualize it, couldn't share it, but what felt like an invisible black wall rushed toward him. A black wall that would swallow everything, and suddenly only one thing mattered anymore.

"I need to go."

3

"You look like you saw a ghost," Nancy Killiam said, the corners of her smile curled into quizzical dimples. She only opened her office door enough to stick her head out.

Bob stared at her and said nothing. He *felt* like a ghost, like a shell of himself. Something had happened, but he wasn't sure what. Impending doom. The black wall of water engulfed his mind, but it wasn't present in any of his external cognitive networks, and Sid assured him it wasn't some game on his part. Bob's cortisol and adrenaline levels had spiked, but not for any physical reason. His friend had investigated, but he hadn't found anything wrong with Bob's systems, either.

But something *was* wrong.

"Are you okay?" Nancy's dimples slipped away, replaced with creases of concern.

"I'm fine," Bob lied. "It's just been a long time," he added, trying to hide the deception.

Nancy knew him better than that. The furrows of concern in her forehead deepened. "*What's* wrong? Something with your family?" She pinged his informational networks, searching. "Something with Sid? Willy?"

"I just needed to see you." This was true. An overpowering desire to see Nancy's face had swelled as the black wall rose around his mind.

It had been a long time since he saw her, at least in person. That was the truth. He continued to stare, inspected the flecked hazel ringing the inside of her blue irises, the sprinkle of freckles across her nose and cheeks. He wanted to scoop her into his arms, felt the sting of losing her as if it was yesterday, but then he was the one who had left her. Or, if not left her, then drifted away.

The furrows of concern wavered and her eyes narrowed. "Are you high?"

"That's insulting."

"Aren't you going to that sensorgy today?" The words dripped with disapproval.

"I . . . uh . . ."

The hazel-flecked eyes twinkled. "I'm kidding. I don't care."

Bob did, though. "Sid wanted to go. You know how he is."

"I know how *you* are." She nodded in a knowing way. "So what's the emergency?"

They stood face-to-face, forty-two floors up in the Cognix tower, at the rented offices of Infinixx Corporation. Nancy's start-up. Whereas Bob had slipped away, insulated himself from the Atopian project, Nancy had embraced it fully. Perhaps all the more so because Bob had rejected it. She was spearheading the development of distributed consciousness for the masses. This was a trick that came naturally to the pssi-kids, but adult brains—which hadn't had the luxury of developing with the pssi-stimulus embedded into them—had a hard time adjusting to distributed consciousness.

Nancy was building the technology that would make it easier for "normal" people to adjust, to make it part of their daily lives as seamlessly as she and the rest of the Atopians now did. The business markets were excited about it, the greatest hope for improving lagging productivity gains in the latter half of the twenty-first century. The plan was to launch Infinixx at the same time as the poly-synthetic sensory interface was launched into the world. Maybe before. That was what he'd heard from Jimmy and his dad.

"I wanted to congratulate you, in person." Bob stuck out his hand. "I heard they moved Infinixx up on the release schedule."

Nancy took his hand but snorted. "And you came physically for that?"

He'd had to navigate through a sea of her minions to get at her core systems, and then past her gatekeeper proxxi, Cunard, to get bumped up the ladder to see her in person. Not long ago, it wouldn't have been like that; he would have been top on her list. He held on to her hand.

"I need to talk to you." Her perfume filled his nostrils, and beneath that, the smell of her. The sense of longing, of not feeling whole, was as overpowering as the blackness that seemed to be everywhere but nowhere.

She tried to pull her hand out of his. "You know I'm busy."

The whole world knew she was busy. He held on. "I can't explain it. I need to talk to you. In person. Privately."

Bob was many things, many of them not good, but he never wasted other people's time. Only his own.

"Now?"

"At the beach."

She exhaled and leaned against her office door, still only half-open. "Give me half an hour. Where?"

"You know where." He released her hand, felt the warmth of it slide out of his.

From here the pounding surf was just a muffled hush, the breathing of the ocean's lungs in and out as it stroked the edges of Atopia. The organic-metal substructure of the mile-wide Atopian platform broke through the sand dunes, near the northern breakwater inlet, where a massive strut rose up to support the circular ring of the passenger cannon five hundred feet overhead. A dense thicket of palms stretched lazily beside the metal cannon strut, their fallen fronds blanketing the sands below. Sea oats swayed on the tops of the dunes toward the sea, and the vivid green Beach Elder shrubs' tiny lavender flowers were blooming, scenting the sea air, while sea grape trees spilled their fruit in ropey bunches.

Their nook was a hidden spot, a place they'd discovered as the first children to grow up on Atopia. Once they had found it, Sid had hidden its existence from the global wikiworld, so it was invisible in the digital realms as well. It was theirs, and nobody else knew about it. Bob still came from time to time, to think, to be alone.

Bob had his dreadlocks tied back. He walked down here himself, not using his proxxi to control his body. Sid pinged his networks, asking when Bob was going to show up at the party. Bob wasn't in the mood for slipping into the virtual worlds but didn't tell Sid this. He just said he was coming and sent his proxxi to cover for him. That was sure to enrage Sid.

While Bob had slid off into his own indulgent world, he hadn't followed the crowd of pssi-kids into their endless virtual worlds. Instead he'd used pssi to enhance his physical body, was obsessed with his physical body, and spent almost all his time in it. The other kids he'd grown up with hardly spent any time at all in their own bodies—most rented them out as psombies, used to do menial labor around the platform, or rented them to tourists. Not Bob. He needed to be in his own skin as much as possible.

"Beautiful, isn't it?" Bob said as Nancy appeared.

He noticed she did her best to ease her way through the Elder shrubs. Her virtual body materialized some way back on the trail. She was busy, her proxxi apologized before Bob could say anything. Latency delays in bringing her physical self out here would delay project deadlines, it continued, but she was bringing her primary subjective conscious stream. Bob didn't need the explanations but appreciated the extra effort.

"That's why we kept it secret," Nancy replied. She stood beside him and watched the waves in the distance.

"Do you think beauty is something that exists independently—"

"You mean Platonic forms?" She shifted from one foot to the other. It was the type of discussion they had used to have here, meandering philosophical talks, wrapped up in each other's arms. She was willing to play along. "That nonphysical forms represent the most accurate description of reality?" It was an old line of discussion from their earliest days of awareness, a philosophical maze that people on the outside indulged on whim, but to pssi-kids, who slipped from one virtual world to another, each as real as the "real" world, it was of more practical importance. "We're only seeing shadows on the cave wall?"

She always could see through him.

"Do you believe that?" he asked. "So what's the reality?"

"I'm more of a believer that beauty is in the mind of the beholder, so only exists in the description of things. Not by itself." The dimples reappeared at the edges of her smile.

"So an idealist."

"'Antirealist' is the more correct term."

"So then the mind constructs reality."

"Of course."

"But do you *really* believe that? Not just words, not just talk. Do you really think it's true?"

"This *reality* is only constructed in our minds." She reached up to grab a bunch of sea grapes, an ironic gesture in a virtual body that wasn't even really there. "Everything we touch, it's not solid. It's just electromagnetic repulsion and attraction, a web of force fields. The actual solid matter of the atoms' cores would fit a mountain into a teaspoon. Human eyes see only specific electromagnetic wave frequencies, our ears hearing only compressed waves in a fluid gas. The understanding and interpretation that created this world are created only deep in the mind. It is only an interpretation of reality. A shadow on a cave wall."

"But the virtual worlds we construct, are they as real as this 'real' world?"

"To us they are."

"That's what I mean. To us. To them. Nothing fixed. We can die in the virtual worlds a million times, but in this world, we die once, and we have no idea what comes next."

"I think we will never know what comes after that."

"So then faith?" Bob kicked the sand. "Why is there this god-shaped hole in people's heads when it—"

She touched his arm the way she did to calm him down. "I'm on your side. What's going on?"

"Information isn't just an abstraction. A single bit of information has a definite energy, just the same as $E=mc^2$ lets us convert energy into mass, the Landauer equations—"

"Two zeta joules, I know."

"It's *real.* As real as this." He kicked the sand up into the air again.

"I love that you're in a philosophical mood"—she dragged one hand through her hair—"but I'm—"

"I love you."

Her head bowed.

"And that's more real than anything," he added.

"Are you sure you're not high?"

"Virtual worlds are not abstractions, they're real things. Or at least have some measure of physical reality to them. So if that's true, then the things we do in them should matter. The things *in* them should matter."

"And I think they do. Everything we do matters in one way or the other."

"Don't patronize me." He edged away. "If the cosmos is an endless maze of infinite parallel universes, where everything that *can* happen *will* happen—what is the point of anything? Why would any one thing be good, and another bad?" As his voice grew louder, Bob splintered bits of his mind into the corners of the Atopian networks where he knew Nancy's cognitive systems were working. To feel her out. See for any unusual spikes in network activity.

"I think you're confusing physicality with morality. What's gotten into you?"

The indulgent smile on Nancy's face had disappeared.

"There's *no* difference, is what I'm saying." The wall of black death in Bob's mind grew higher, grew deeper. He needed something, anything. "I need to know what—"

"I've had enough of this."

Bob hadn't been careful in sending out his agents. Her security settings had changed. She sensed him sensing her. Invading her space. She still stood in front of him, in her virtual self, but her primary subjective had already left, leaving behind a vacant-minded splinter to mop up the rest of whatever Bob was rambling about. She was busy was the unsaid subtext, so stop wasting her time. He withdrew his agents, despite an urge to send more.

"Thanks for coming," he said through a sigh.

"We'll talk later." Even the splinter looked annoyed as it signed off. It didn't even bother to wade off through the Elder shrubs, but dematerialized before his eyes.

"Excellent questions, my friend."

The rasping voice reverberated through Bob's cognitive systems, but there was nothing in his audio channels. This voice wasn't compression waves in the air. It was an agency deep in his mind. An intrusion. He scanned his visual fields, shut down his network access points, and laid honey traps along the neurons leading into his auditory nerves, but there was nothing.

A hooded figure emerged from the thicket of palms away from the dunes.

Bob quickened his nervous system, amped up the electrical conductivity along his neurons and axons, flushing his bloodstream with adrenaline. This intruder didn't show up on any of his wikiworld feeds, was invisible to his digital visual overlays, didn't even appear in his biological sensory organs. It only appeared somewhere deep within his mind, and yet there it was—*he* was—something not there but there. A translucent, gray security blanket descended around them in the local digital space.

"Don't bother," said the hooded figure.

Bob turned from the dappled sunshine and into the shade, retreating from the figure. He'd been about to launch a counteroffensive and contact Sid. Maybe this was another one of his friend's perverse attempts at humor. No metatags, no information of any kind. Robert, Bob's proxxi, tried to contact him, but a splinter emerged from Bob's own mind and told him it was okay, that he was just feeling nervous about Nancy.

This thing had hijacked Bob's pssi-controls, had infiltrated his deepest inner networks. He'd lost control.

"Who are you?" Bob asked.

"Information."

"What does that mean?"

"I am a shadow, like you said, against the wall of Plato's cave. You can call me Shadow."

Still nothing was being recorded in Bob's inVerse. It was as if this wasn't happening. No record of any kind except what was deep inside his mind. Could he pull it back out? If it wasn't recorded, did it even exist? *Was* he high?

"If a tree falls in the forest, another very old question," the Shadow said, reading his thoughts.

"You said you are information. What kind?" It was obvious this thing wanted something. Bob needed to buy time.

"The kind that will save everyone's life."

"And *who* is everyone?"

"Another excellent question."

This was some new form of technology, beyond Atopian. "Are you from Terra Nova?" The rivalry between the two competing seastead giants had intensified. The media ratcheted things up into a frenzy, and Atopia didn't shy away from it. Any publicity was good publicity.

The Shadow's head dipped. "I am from everywhere and nowhere."

How was this possible? How had this intruder breached Bob's internal networks without so much as raising an alarm? "I can't help you."

"I think you can."

"Let me rephrase. I will *not* help you."

"But you already have."

Bob shattered his mind into fragments, tried to pierce the glittering blanket, but every attempt failed. It wasn't even a contest, his efforts mites in the face of a hurricane. "So that was you? The dark wall? What I felt?"

The Shadow paused. "She is different, but the same. This *place* is different. I have waited for time beyond measuring, beyond your comprehension . . ."

It was no use resisting. "What do you want?" Whatever happened, Bob needed to escape first. He could alert the Atopian border authorities afterward, but right now he needed to get away from this thing.

"I need to know *how* this place is different."

"From what?" Bob still struggled, smothered inside the black security blanket that tightened around him. "And why should I help you?" He needed all the information he could get.

Beyond the dark blanket, Bob sensed the infinite black wall pressing in.

"I will show you all," groaned the Shadow.

Irresistible, the blackness flowed into Bob's mind. Not empty, though, it was filled with images, of places and people, of things past and gone.

4

Shafts of sunlight stabbed into the depths, illuminating a mass of tiny phosphorescent creatures. They didn't float, but danced, jammed, to the beat of a faraway voice. The watery depths had no end, for these were seas of the virtual oceans, a construction beyond the Looking Glass. Bob forced his mind to focus, to resist slipping into the other projections of this world, to the synesthetic, formless blobs coalescing and merging splintered parts of chemically and digitally distorted minds.

This world wasn't meant to be experienced straight.

Just to get in, Bob had to prove to the world's gatekeepers that he'd ingested synthetic ketamine, and Sid refused to let any parts of his cognitive networks converse unless Bob refracted through the Looking Glass first. Bob had no choice, and Sid could be obstinate. Especially when he wanted to get high.

The mass of dancing creatures gained some form, the individuals separating. Bob wriggled his tentacles at full force to propel himself through the brine. Glowing squidworms entangled one another in amorous wrestling while sea dragons and siphonophores watched—a retroluminescent aquatic party. One worm stood out, stood apart, its metatags glowing brighter than the jellyfish trying to mate with it.

"Sid," said Bob.

"Bob?" said Sid, his metatags flickering over his worm-form.

"Goddamn it, I need your help."

"You promised," giggled the worm. Two of the jellyfish wrapped their tentacles around the worm, sucking it into their mouth-parts. The worm trembled.

Bob's tentacles spasmed in frustration. He barreled blob-first into the nearest jelly and sent it sprawling into the depths. The other released the worm. Its tentacles pulsed in confusion. Bob pulled a glittering green security blanket around them.

"You promised," repeated Sid-worm. "For weeks you said you'd ditch your surfboard and come past the Looking Glass with me to the sensorgy, so I'm sorry if I had to drag your amoebic ass—"

"I need to hack into Cognix . . ."

Sid-worm continued unaware: "—down here, but you got here just before the slingshot—"

"To hack into Patricia Killiam's accounts."

The worm quit wriggling. Its bioluminescence blinked on and off, on and off. "What?"

"You heard me."

"When?"

"Now."

"Before the slingshot test?"

Bob-amoeba expanded and contracted to say yes.

"And did you say Patricia *Killiam*?"

"I can't tell you why."

"Are you insane?"

"Maybe." The thought had crossed Bob's mind. More than once.

"Because I like it." Sid-worm glowed bright. "You know we could get into a heap of trouble for—"

"I know."

"*And* it's your brother's birthday tomorr—"

"Don't remind me."

The worm glowed ever more luminescent. "I'm in. Let's get out of here." Sid-worm wriggled upward, toward the light, but stopped. "One thing."

"What's that?"

"I'm incredibly high."

"Then you might not remember later." Which was fine with Bob.

His only ally in the fight against Death was a stoned nematode.

"You're the one that wanted me to get involved." Bob perched on the edge of the copper-studded leather attending chair in Patricia Killiam's private synthetic space office. A bottle-green lampshade glowed over her mahogany desk, and a wall of dog-eared books framed her pale wrinkled face as she eased back in her chair. The hallways leading in and out of this projection were lined with oil paintings of sail-rigged ships in flames and men on horses charging into battle.

"But conscious transference? Your specialty is metasensory overlays."

Bob shrugged, nonplussed. "That doesn't interest me anymore. *You* always said we had to follow our interests." He'd forgone his outfit of boarding shorts and instead had his virtual presence smartly dressed in khakis and a button-down long-sleeved shirt. That alone inspired a level of suspicion that Bob was well aware of.

Patricia regarded him with the appropriate level of dubiousness. "Right now isn't a good time."

She checked her watch to illustrate the point, a body language gesture Bob was only able to interpret by checking historical archives.

"Okay." He shrugged again to make his point that he didn't care. In any negotiation, you needed a walk-away option, *and* to be prepared to play it. He began to dematerialize, but slowly, wincing on the inside but smiling languidly without.

"I'll have to ask Jimmy." Patricia relented, distrustful but seeing the opportunity he knew she was looking for.

Bob hung halfway in and halfway out of her world. "But you'll give me access?"

"I will."

He allowed his body to regain some definition. "Can I choose other projects?"

She checked her watch again, and without asking pulled their viewpoint into the Atopian Defense Force command. The sleek white lines of the control hub hovered just outside a crackling pale-blue security blanket that Patricia kept their conversation wrapped inside. Commander Rick Strong stood in the middle of the room, his face a study in controlled tension. The slingshot weapons battery was about to be tested for the first time, unleashing its awesome power. The world's media was tuned into the event, and Bob watched Patricia talk to a virtual meeting room full of reporters, then begin ferrying their viewpoints up into the edge of space to watch the test start.

Patricia's secondary subjective continued the conversation with him: "What other projects?"

"I'll continue with the metasense projects if you like."

"And that's it?"

"And maybe the Synthetic Beings Charter of Rights."

"SyBCoR?" Patricia's eyebrows twitched up.

Her proxxi, Marie, materialized into the conversation space with them. Patricia's proxxi was the very first under the pssi protocol and held an archangel position in the hierarchy of digital intelligences. She didn't say anything, but eyed Bob, then nodded at Patricia.

"I'll have to review all this in my primary, but yes," said Patricia.

"And the POND, I'm curious about that as well." He'd waited until the end, added this as an afterthought. Tried to make the appearance of this being a casual reference, but he wasn't well versed in deception. "I'd really like to look at the data," he added, which was the truth.

Did it work?

Patricia eyed him steadily, but her primary subjective snapped back into this instance of her the moment he mentioned the Pacific Ocean Neutrino Detector. “Why?” she asked.

Patricia continued to watch Bob. In that fraction of a second, he completed the thoughts, his ideas, and she relented, needing to get back to her reporters. She gave him access to her networks, but seemed to want to keep him close. Her digital agents dispatched into Bob’s own systems, to watch him.

“Did you get that?” Bob whispered to Sid on a side channel. The conversation space with Patricia faded.

“We’re connected,” Sid confirmed. “Are you going to tell me why yet?”

Bob held his virtual viewpoint at a hundred thousand feet above sea level, five miles west of Atopia. The seastead glittered below, an emerald pinpoint of glass towers swallowed in the Pacific wilderness. The thin white wisp of the lower atmosphere painted a feathered edge onto the curve of the horizon, the sky a purple blue, the pinpricks of stars just beginning to pierce it—at this altitude—even in midday. Patricia’s collection of reporters hovered in their virtual point-of-presence nearby. Everyone waited for the show to start.

A mile away, a flash, and then another, and then a stuttering burst of explosions that grew into a wall of glowing plasma. A high-altitude UAV, its gossamer wings—covered in photo-cells—shimmering, tried to bank away from the blossoming fireball but had ventured too close. Some kind of malfunction.

“I saved him,” the Shadow said. “Your friend Vincent Indigo. He was to be in that UAV, trying to escape.”

"So you say." Bob saw the phutures the Shadow predicted, his friend Vince scrambling to escape his future by hiding in the UAV, using the cover of the slingshot test to hide his exit.

"You think I am lying?"

"I don't know what to think."

"And yet you are breaking into Cognix, hacking Patricia's networks."

"Not me. Sid."

"At your request."

"At your insistence."

Less than a day had passed since the Shadow had inserted itself into Bob's networks, but it seemed an eternity. Deep in the sky, beyond his natural optical range but highlighted in his visual overlays, the comet Wormwood was passing Jupiter's orbit. In just weeks the comet's tail would be visible to the naked eye.

"Another way this world may end," the Shadow said, seeing Bob's mind wander upward.

"All worlds end."

"You don't believe me."

The slingshot's plasma shield expanded before them, now miles in blistering width.

The Shadow had shared its information, secrets it said were encoded in the POND data Patricia had already intercepted, but not yet decoded. Patricia's teams had only partially deciphered it, a warning to Atopia, to stop its virtual reality program—that what it was creating was more than simply virtual.

"Something happened in this place, or a place very much like it," the Shadow said. "Something escaped into the multiverse. Something from Atopia—a *thing* that became the Destroyer of worlds."

The Shadow hadn't shared all its information, but already this was more than Bob wanted. His mind filled with images of a hooded priest wandering across sand dunes. "And where is this priest?" Bob asked. "Show me. We are here now. Show me this Destroyer."

"In my world"—the Shadow eased out these words in a whisper—"he only appeared after the secrets of Terra Nova were revealed." The Shadow paused, its image expanded and contracted, both visible and not visible over the fireball of the slingshot's plasma shield. "But it is here, watching. I am certain. If I reveal my existence—that I have crossed over—it will destroy this world as well. I have watched it happen, over and over. Look in the POND data, when Patricia gives you access. Use the key I have given you. You must trust me."

But Bob already saw.

In Patricia's tiny hesitations when he had mentioned the POND, he saw fear.

In the information the Shadow had given him, he saw the hurricanes winding up the coast of Mexico, already pushing Commander Strong's team to wheel Atopia closer to the border of America. The hurricanes didn't exist; they were just reality-skin infections implanted by Terra Nova, the competing offshore colony, to try to bring about the destruction of Atopia. The Shadow was right. Bob saw the deception of Patricia and Kesselring, chasing his friend Vince Indigo around with the phuture reality infection. A massive part of the computing infrastructure of Cognix was devoted to this, but to what end? To hide the obvious, that Kesselring and Killiam were planning to hook the world on the virtual crack cocaine of their pssi interface, that they were going to give it away for free to start with, like digital drug pushers.

The deception took Bob's breath away.

In a day, his world had changed. The Shadow wanted him to root through Atopia, to discover the identity of the Destroyer, to find out what had happened. To stop the destruction from happening again.

5

The royal banners snapped in a sudden wind. The squall raised spirals of dust devils on the distant plains where the Tatars amassed. Dark clouds threatened, their shadows blotted across the landscape. The fight today would be bloody and muddy, just the way Bob usually liked it.

Bob balanced his saber across his knees and tried to keep them from jittering up and down. He must have looked nervous. He *was* nervous, but it wasn't for the coming fight. With one hand he smoothed his pencil-thin mustache, dragged his fingers across his olive-brown skin and down the chain-mail armor over his chest. Mongol warriors led their horses past and stole quick glances at their leader, Temüjin, the whispers already spreading through the camps of his ascension to the status of Genghis Khan, the Universal Ruler.

"Do you ever get the feeling that none of this is real?" Martin asked. He sat to the right of Bob with a bloody deer haunch in his hand that he circled as punctuation to the question.

And usually this sort of question would elicit a groan from Bob, followed by a complaint that his brother, Martin—who was already dead, although Martin didn't know it—was ruining the afternoon's game of Asian Invasion. The irony of the question wasn't lost today, wasn't consumed in the frothy nonsensical ocean of virtual gameworlds.

"You know what I mean," Martin continued. "I mean, how can I know that I really exist?"

You don't exist, Bob thought but didn't say. Why didn't he say anything? Because it would be cruel, would inflict pain upon this digital creature that thought he was Bob's dead brother.

"You can't ever *really* know," he replied to Martin's question, his guttural Mongol voice struggling with the philosophical banter. "I think, therefore I am, as Descartes famously put it in 1644. Since then, not much progress." Bob winced as the words came out, the overpowering sense of déjà vu—of being there before—fighting the black walls that pressed against the edges of his mind.

This sort of answer was a clever response to help move the game along, to quell Martin's mind and get him focused, but all Bob could think was, how *could* he know if he really existed? He knew this world wasn't real, that it was just a digitally constructed gameworld instantiated a few days ago when Bob and Sid had decided to invade Crimea again.

The warriors leading their horses past him, these artificial intelligences endowed with just enough cognitive powers to enable them to act and react realistically in their roles—did *they* know that they weren't real? They *thought*, so therefore *were* they real? What did "real" mean? It was a distinction lost on many pssi-kids.

Martin smiled and wiped his greasy face with the back of one hand, and was about to ask another question when Vicious—Sid's proxxi—rode up on a white stallion, his knobby knees poking out from under the Mongol battle armor. "Your 'orses are ready."

Robert rode behind Vicious and led the two horses. Bob sheathed his saber, and Martin dropped his deer haunch.

Bob swung himself onto his stead, felt the familiar grip of the Mongol saddle. He'd been taught to ride at the age of two by his mother, Hoelun, wife of the chief of the Khamag confederation. Even from a young age, there had been high expectations. She'd tied him to the saddle on his first ride at thirty months of age, strapped him tight so he wouldn't fall as she sent the horse at a gallop across the plains. He remembered the fear but also the excitement—the pungent horsehair caught in his mouth, the wind ripping at his knot of hair, and his mother pulling him off the horse, the tang of her perfume, the warmth of her breast as his lungs pulled air in and out.

All these memories were implanted into his external cognition networks, a part of the game engine that created this world and these characters. It was so easy to slip into another sensory space—real or virtual—that Bob had almost forgotten how strange a thing it was to inhabit someone else's body.

He had become this Mongol warlord and could get lost if he allowed himself. Yet he knew he wasn't this person. He could die here, in the coming battle with Tatars, but he knew he would revert to his physical body on Atopia or some other virtual body in another gameworld. He could die a million times out here—a billion times—yet he could not die in the real world, in the identity universe.

Or could he?

Nobody knew what happened when humans died in the real world. It was a veil that couldn't be punctured, not except by faith, and Bob hated the god-shaped hole that seemed to exist in people's heads when they talked about death and faith and the afterlife. There was no afterlife. This was all there was. But what was *this*?

"You ready?" Sid trotted up to him on his own horse. "You're the one that said you wanted to do this."

"I'm ready."

They followed Martin's horse through the encampment. The smoke of cooking fires rose between the yurts, drifted on the wind. The year was 1198, at the battle where Temüjin ascended to the leadership of the Horde. Sid had suggested getting their gang together for this game weeks ago, had set all the parameters, but he was surprised when Bob hadn't canceled this morning. He'd assumed that after they'd hacked into the Cognix networks, sapped their way into the POND data as Bob had asked, that other things might be more important.

Another battle was being waged now.

A bigger game was afoot.

The Shadow wanted Bob to hunt down Death, and for the moment, they needed to keep everything looking normal. Which meant playing the gameworlds.

Bob slipped into his Mongol identity. "Have we prepared the decoys?" he asked Sid, his second in command, who inhabited the body of the Mongol general Subutai.

"On the horizon." Sid-Subutai pointed into the distance.

A cloud of dust. A thousand horses with men atop them crested the hills—except those weren't men. They were stuffed dummies, tied to the horses, a thousand new mannequin cavalry led by a dozen boys not more than ten years of age each. Even a thousand years ago, simulations were important in winning battles.

Bob-Khan felt a rush of pleasure imagining the fear the appearance of this new Mongol force must be inspiring in the Tatars just preparing for battle. The dread. The Mongols were outnumbered by more than two to one, but in this battle, they would send in the dummy cavalry first, which the Tatars would meet with their own. The Mongol warriors would hold back and send volley after volley of light long-range arrows into the melee as the two forces met.

Which would inspire more terror.

That the Mongol were firing on their own men.

This was part of the tactics that had begun long before this battle. The campaign of terror, of psychological warfare to demoralize the troops of the enemy. Even outnumbered two to one, the Mongol army had the advantage. Each warrior was an independent unit, a fighting force unto his or her own, who had expert knowledge of the local culture, vegetation, and most important, water supplies. It had taken a week's hard ride to meet this enemy force, to rout them before they could meet up with another army coming from the south. In that week, the Khan's army had barely eaten, and many had resorted to drinking the blood of their horses.

This was the Mongol Horde.

There was no defeating it.

"We are ready," Sid-Subutai said. "We attack at your command."

Subutai had been the Khan's primary military strategist. He had the distinction of being the military commander who had conquered more territory than any other soldier in history—his record of defeating thirty-two nations and winning sixty-five pitched battles still survived into modern times, a record that had stood for over a thousand years and would probably never be matched. He had once defeated the armies of Poland and Hungary in two days of each other, battles five hundred kilometers apart.

Sid-Subutai was the master of strategy, and Bob needed him. In this world or any other.

Before him, Bob-Khan's army quivered in anticipation.

To act, or not to act—these were both decisions. Bob had played along with the Shadow, this mysterious interloper, trying to figure out what was going on. He could do nothing, but doing nothing might threaten this Shadow seeping deeper into his own networks. He couldn't lock it out, not by himself, and the threat felt real—the dark wall of doom that seemed to permeate everything since the Shadow's arrival.

"Sir?" Sid-Subutai reined back his horse, sent it skittering around in a tight circle. It sensed the blood coming.

"Now!" Bob unsheathed his saber and charged forward.

His army roared and followed.

High in the clear sky, vultures wheeled and waited for the meat-piles of dead men to be stacked and left alone for their dinner. The Tatar fortification burned on the horizon, and a black smudge of smoke rose up over it, a signal of fear to the army advancing from the south to stay away. Already, Subutai had dispatched spies to spread rumors of the Mongols eating the captured, resuming his campaign of terror for the next conquest.

Bob-Khan had washed away the blood from the fight and sat, perfumed and clothed in red-and-gold silks, in a mass of pillows outside in the shade of the royal yurt, with a view over the battlefield. Sid-Subutai sat with him, a glass of koumiss—fermented mare's milk—in his hand. A glittering blue security blanket surrounded them. The Khan had requested that nobody come within earshot, on pain of death—very painful death. He needed a private talk with his master strategist.

"Maybe it's Patricia," Sid-Subutai said. "She's been wanting to get you back into working at the research center. Now she's got her wish. Simple." He took a long drink from the koumiss. "A do-gooder trying to save the world, reduce its pain and suffering. Sounds like your Destroyer to me. Teaching you a lesson."

"Reduce pain and suffering? By destroying?" The Shadow had specifically instructed Bob not to tell Sid about its existence, or the existence of the Destroyer, but the best defense was always a good offense. Keep the enemy off balance, and Sid was his best offensive weapon—in all ways.

"Of course," Sid replied. "Suffering only exists if a thing exists. Wipe out the thing, and you wipe out the suffering."

Bob hadn't thought of it like that. This sounded a lot like the discussion of forms he'd had with Nancy. Did suffering exist independent of a mind or description? Or did it only exist when suffering things existed? Or was it something constructed solely in the mind, only existing as a description of a thing in suffering? "That sounds like suicide."

One of Sid-Subutai's eyebrows raised high. "Mercy killing is more like it."

"You're being awfully glib about this."

"I'm not the one being hunted by his shadow," Sid replied. "That, plus it's bullshit."

"This thing is real."

"So you say, but I can't find any evidence of you talking to it in your inVerse."

After the battle, Bob made his decision. Or perhaps he made it during the battle as he felt the thrill of killing and victory. Whatever he thought of this Shadow entity, the information it provided was real enough. Something was going on inside of Atopia, and he and Sid were going to get to the bottom of it. Once he had explained everything he knew to Sid, they'd cast a wide net to try to capture evidence of the Shadow, but so far—nothing. "Whatever it is, it's erasing its tracks."

"It's not erasing—not unless it's a far more sophisticated technology than I can understand. Erasing would leave telltale signatures. I've got an easier explanation."

"And that is?"

"You've lost your mind."

Bob-Khan tried not to be incensed at his general's insolence. "For the sake of argument, can we—"

"Yeah, yeah."

Now Bob-Khan had to resist his Mongol instinct to cleave Sid-Subutai in half.

His subordinate relented. "So this thing is from the future?"

"And the past."

"Then tell it to give me next week's Power Lotto numbers in America. The jackpot's up to sixteen billion dollars. With all that cash we—"

"Can you be serious? I've shown you the reality-skin infection, the simulated hurricanes. Something is trying to destroy Atopia, and it's going to implicate *you*."

"I *am* being serious." Sid took another sip of his koumiss. "So it says that some type of being—"

"Some*one*."

"—escaped from Atopia, using the pssi system—"

"It calls it nervenet."

"—using a nervenet to escape into the physical multiverse. How the hell does that work?"

"It hasn't told me everything yet. But for the sake—"

"Maybe Kesselring? He's a nutbar bent on total control."

"I'm thinking Patricia," Bob replied. "That's who the Shadow sent me to first. Her plan is to release pssi and send everyone into virtual slavery."

"To reduce the planet's suffering."

"Exactly." The great Genghis paused. "This Shadow says that Jimmy kills Patricia, that he killed his parents. The Destroyer infected him."

"Doesn't everyone die in your friend's story?"

"This thing isn't my friend."

"Seems like it's trying to be." Sid lost his impish grin, replaced it with a grim blankness. "What about Terra Nova? They're the ones that implanted this reality-skin hurricane to destroy Atopia. Maybe this is another step up in an ongoing battle."

"So Tyrel and Mohesha? They're the leaders of Terra Nova. That could make some sense. They're kind of hippie-dangerous."

Bob-Khan agreed.

"But if you're looking for dangerous," Sid-Subutai continued, "what about the Russian gangster Mikhail Butorin? If anything dangerous would have escaped into the world, I'd bet on that creepy asshole."

They'd tracked his mandroid, Susan, which had already been granted access to Atopia by Patricia. What hold did Butorin have over Patricia? Why did she grant the mandroid access, when she clearly knew this thing was an agent of his? Images of the creature, with its meat-stump of a body suspended in the air atop spindly metal legs, flitted between the two friends.

"And Vince Indigo," Bob-Khan said. "The Shadow saved his life yesterday. It stopped him from getting into the UAV that was destroyed in the slingshot test."

"So you suspect Vince?" Sid-Subutai's forehead creased in angry red furrows. "Then what about me?"

They eyed each other.

"Or me," Bob said, his voice quiet. "It said that I was the one who made it possible for the Destroyer to obliterate the world."

"The same as Jimmy and everyone else in that fairytale," his friend countered. "Have you told Nancy?"

"This Shadow thing was very"—Bob paused to find the right word—"persuasive about me not revealing anything about its existence. I couldn't risk it."

"But you could risk me." Sid-Subutai's impish grin returned. He unsheathed his dagger and drew a line in the sand at his feet. "What we need to do is eliminate the actors in this play, one by one. Like one of those old detective films. Box them in, so they can't—"

The glittering security blanket surrounding them sparkled; an effervescent shimmering snow of electricity danced around the circumference of its dome.

"What the hell is—"

Mountains of dead bodies stacked into the distance folded into the earth, the sky circling down and around to swallow the ground, leaving a rushing dead blackness that pulled every neuron and fiber.

"I told you . . ." A voice of crushed ice and gravel. "What have you done?"

The Shadow emerged from the blackness and loomed over Bob and Sid, their corporeal forms lost in the dimensionless space left behind after the gameworld collapsed into a singularity.

"Holy—" Sid grabbed Bob's digital presence and tried to drag it away, back to the world. "This thing isn't registering on any of my sensory channels."

"What have you done?" repeated the Shadow. Its hooded figure grew over them.

"I told you," Bob whispered on a subtext channel to Sid. He didn't bother to resist.

Instead of delivering a message or trying to communicate, the Shadow shared an image, of a white-lab-coated scientist in Brookhaven Lab in Connecticut. Behind the woman loomed a massive machine, a zettawatt laser of a design neither Bob nor Sid had ever seen, seemingly beyond technical possibility. The machine was powering up, glowing hot blue.

"Shit." Sid's cognition systems processed the same data as the Shadow sent to Bob.

In a fraction of a second, the laser would fire two opposing pulses into an ignition target, a femtosecond pulse, and this wouldn't just ignite a fusion sequence. The Shadow had seen it before. It dug deep into Bob's cognition systems in an instant, tore all his memories out, and fused them with its own. It took hold of the world's communications infrastructure, satellites, and radio dishes, and fired off a stream of its data.

The laser fired, igniting the target, initiating the event.

A millionth of a second later, the Earth was gone.

6

The Engineer swung her virtual viewpoint around the peripheries of her creation, the Project now complete in its full glory encircling this hot blue star. Thousands of ignition-point collectors rimmed the sphere of photonic arrays, and she cycled through each of them, focused the energy of the star into a cylindrical funnel barely the width of a hair, but to her nanoscale robotics this was as wide as an ocean. Each collector hummed to life, glimmered with its sheath of negative energy, the tiny probes balanced on the edge of reality.

Her journey had begun so long ago, it was hard to believe it was all about to end.

Did she feel fear?

Not fear. Something else.

Almost six hundred years before, she had been among the first to push their primitive computing technology beyond mere number crunching and into the realm of self-awareness. At the same time, in lock-step, she'd helped create the first sensory-realistic virtual technology, what she'd called the nervenet. A synthesized reality that was indistinguishable from physical reality, that created the same sensory inputs to neurons, the same perception of the "world" created deep within the seat of the mind.

"Check the wave front again," the Engineer said to her doppelgänger, her synthesized twin.

A young Umebak woman materialized into a shared meeting space—green-hued skin with beautiful, smooth ventral lobes. Four arms raised, and one morphed into a hand and spread three fingers. "I see no issues, Engineer." Even five hundred years after departing from their biological forms, they still kept using them in synthetic spaces.

The Engineer checked the data herself. One and then the next of the qubit probes came up the same, exactly on the wave front of the approaching meta-stability event. It had reached the outer edges of this star system. In three hours, the Project would be wiped from existence, but three hours was an eternity. More than enough time for her to escape, or at least parts of her.

For there was nothing solid about physical reality. It was a sensory perception of electromagnetic waves, electrostatic force fields. What did it matter if one set of electrical forces was exchanged for another, delivered from the computations of a created machine? The seat of the mind still perceived it the same, the physical laws of these created universes governed by the creators. The machines themselves were natural creations of natural animals—a machine gun was no less natural than a termite mound. There was nothing artificial about the created realities of the nervenet, when the neural machinery of minds slipped away from biological to computational substrates.

As the biological basis of the Umebaks' collective minds had slipped away—their thoughts and memories reproduced in ever-advancing computing machinery—their bodies' sensory networks had grown to encompass whole physical worlds and endless digital universes. The development of the Engineer's nervenet was the chrysalis that transformed the Umebak from fragile planet-bound bags of water and protein into timeless godlike beings that spanned star systems.

It was also the moment the Engineer had first felt the *presence.*

At first the *presence* was, perhaps, felt only as an inspiration. In what seemed an eternity of time before, it had guided her to saving the Umebak race in its first skirmishes with self-extinction. The *presence* had helped her develop the technologies that enabled them to rise from their homeworld, to reach out into the stars. It let her see solutions that nobody else could see, to build the computronium matrices into the expanding communication sphere, creating unending virtual worlds that the biological and informational spawn of the Umebak disappeared into. This power made it possible for her to install her spy network, to monitor the Umebak—to see into the future.

For she was not only Engineer—many called her Prophet.

For the *presence* was not benign, not just a guardian angel—it was also a demon. She used it to crush opposition, to inspire fear, to put down rebellions. She had her own fear of it, as well, but it had saved her and her people so many times that it inspired a kind of trust. And it was the wellspring for the fear that held the Vollix Hardadiss in place—but the Vollix would not be denied much longer. She'd made too many concessions. With the end approaching, she sensed this was a battle that had been fought for time beyond measure.

And not just in this world.

The Project was a machine that could puncture the fabric of space and time but would not break the speed of causality. Once a wormhole was opened, information was still bound by this speed limit; it merely had a shorter pathway to exploit, but the technology to create negative energy could be used to create weapons of almost unimaginable violence, and deliver them anywhere within the universe—and perhaps beyond, perhaps even to end this universe. So the Engineer kept her mind compartmentalized, kept some of the secrets of the machine hidden even from herself.

She didn't even know what was in the probes.

Only the *presence* knew.

7

The flash point of creation, unending fireworks in higher-dimensional space, staccato gunfire in the dark of infinity.

In the beginning, there was no light—only a sub-atomic pinprick of unimaginable black heat, but for the first fractional instants, it expanded within the speed of causality. For the first instants, each part of itself was able to speak to the other.

A trillionth of a trillionth of a second after creation, the furious pinpoint expanded from sub-atomic to the size of a golf ball at a speed trillions of times faster than the speed of light, beyond the speed of causality, and information could no longer pass from one side of this newly created bubble of reality to the other. The strong and weak nuclear forces separated from each other and from electromagnetism and gravity, the initial creational conditions laying down a network of myriad parameters, the physical laws governing this new universe. Expansion slowed to the speed of causality, and the edges of this reality became forever isolated from one another. The initial conditions set, a chain of actions, forever unbreakable, was set in motion.

One second after creation, the universe filled with a soup of sub-atomic particles—neutrons, protons, electrons, and a flood of neutrinos. After five minutes, the first atomic nuclei formed as the temperature cooled to a billion degrees. For four hundred thousand years, the bubble expanded and cooled, the heat of creation pressing out until—

And then there was light.

A burst of microwave radiation showered into space as the first elements coalesced from the soup of particles, a bright echo imprinted forever on the background of this nubile universe. This burst of photons scuttled into the vastness as the elemental soup settled, and this cosmos was plunged back into darkness for a half-billion years more, until the clouds of gases clumped into masses large enough for their collective gravity to press them together with enough force to ignite nuclear fusion.

The first stars were born, casting the second wave of light into the darkness.

Simple balls of helium and hydrogen, the first stars were formed in pairs or triplets, some with gaseous companions that failed to reach densities high enough for self-ignition—but no rocky planets. No elements more dense than traces of lithium existed yet. Over billions of years, these first stars burned through their fuel, fusing hydrogen into helium, then helium into heavier elements, became bloated, and in a final act imploded and exploded, showering the cosmos with clouds of gases, again mostly helium and hydrogen, but also heavier elements—carbon, oxygen, and more.

Wave after wave of stars was born and died. Massive black holes formed halos of them, the galaxies birthed, and from this something new—rocky planets began to form around the new stars. Awash in fragments of ice, these new star systems plunged through their own creation throes, and on uncounted worlds, something else.

Life.

Self-replicating strands of information—some newly formed, some gleaned from the interstellar dust—wriggled and reformed using the energy cast from the fusion of the fiery orbs. Over billions more years, they learned to sense their environment, to find food to fuel their growth, competing to survive. Convergent evolution forced over again and again the genesis of tentacles, of grippers and hands, and of eyes. Millions and then trillions of worlds, life dissimilar yet the same.

And on countless more worlds, something new again.

Intelligence.

♦◆♦

"You look like you saw a ghost." Nancy Killiam stared with welcome bemusement at Bob.

He held her gaze carefully, wanted to pull her into his arms, but dread tingled across his scalp. A black wall of infinity rose up around his mind. What had just happened? More specifically, what had just happened to *him*? A second ago he had been . . . what? Surfing? No, he'd been talking with Sid, but that wasn't quite right. He had to fight his way back into his body, to regain control from his proxxi—who was unusually quiet now.

"Are you okay?" his estranged girlfriend asked. The merry twinkle in her eyes subsided.

"I'm just . . ." The air seemed to suck itself from his lungs. He took two quick breaths to steady himself.

"Bob, what's wr—"

"Come and meet me, down at the beach."

Nancy's avatar materialized in the shade of the palmettos and walked out to join Bob. He stared at the waves breaking on the beach in the distance. The organic-metal substructure of the mile-wide Atopian platform broke through the sand dunes here where this massive strut rose up to support the circular ring of the passenger cannon five hundred feet overhead. Seagrass swayed.

Their secret place.

One of them.

"Are we *real*?" Bob said without explanation.

"Are you *stoned*?" She sighed, loud enough for him to hear it. "I'm busy. You know how busy I am." She had sent her primary subjective, still deemed him important enough for this, and Bob acknowledged it.

"I'm not kidding," he persisted.

"Are you *sure* you're not stoned?" she asked again.

A valid question despite its annoyance. He'd spent most of the last five years bending his physical and digital minds under the weight of personality-dissociative drugs, a self-induced stupor of indulgence. "How can we know?"

Nancy took a long look at him before she settled her digital self onto an outcropping of rock near the passenger cannon's support. "It's an old problem. Plato was one of the first to put it forward two thousand years ago. That we're not living in the real world. That we're shadow creatures on a cave wall and the real world casting the shadows is somewhere else. Out there. Beyond."

Shadow creatures: the words gave Bob a chill. Fear frosted over the unease already settled into the churned lining of his stomach. Something inside struggled to get out, fought him for control of his corporeal systems—a splinter of his consciousness tried to worm its way to the surface. He suppressed it.

"Punch your Uncle Button," Nancy suggested. "If that's what you're afraid of. Do it now."

Every person with Atopian pssi was trained in how to trigger their system reset, the so-called Uncle Button. It disconnected external stimuli, put your own brain back into control of your body, and pulled your sensory systems back into their normalized neuronal states. No matter where you were or what you were doing or who had control, this was a hardwired failsafe built deep into the core.

"I have. I did. Nothing happens."

"So you're safe." She brushed sand from her leg. "At least, as safe as safe can be."

"But what if all this isn't real?"

"Then just try and do good things, so whoever is running the simulation doesn't turn it off." Nancy stood to dust more sand off her legs, trying not to make it too obvious that she moved closer to Bob. "Is this really why you barged in on me today? It's been a long time."

Longer than she could possibly imagine. Bob's external cognition networks jammed with a new flood of images, of suns being born and dying, of civilizations rising and falling into the dust. Millions of years flashed before his mind, boxes unfolded into larger boxes into a mirror maze of dimensions. What was happening to him? He pushed the splinter away, the one still trying to surface into his primary consciousness. "Do you think we're doomed to repeat the past?"

"Is that what this is about?" She put an arm around him, a gesture at once too familiar and too remote. "You can't blame yourself for your brother."

"What if I've done something . . ." He pulled away. "Something . . . something *so* bad."

She let him pull away without resisting. "What could be so bad?" Her voice barely a whisper over the hiss of the sand carried through the dunes.

An awkward silence settled in the valleys between their words.

"First, before anything else," Nancy said softly, "you've got to love yourself. Everything comes from that. You can't help anyone else until you love yourself first."

"I hate myself."

"Love overcomes hate. It always does. Even when it doesn't." She didn't really smile, but the corners of her mouth raised in a tremble.

His systems were overloading. His cognition networks flooded and overflowed. "I need to strip myself clean."

Now she laughed. "That is never a bad idea."

"I'm being serious."

"So am I." She pulled his chin around. "Look at me."

And he did.

Into her clear blue eyes.

But.

They weren't *her* eyes.

Before they dated, he'd had a crush on her, had spent whole afternoons—whole *weeks*—obsessing over Nancy's eyes, the flecks of hazel at the center, the way the edges changed from green to blue on clear days when they went topside to the beaches. The eyes of the woman staring back at him were pale blue. No flecks of hazel.

"What's wrong?"

Bob recoiled involuntarily, shoved her away. "I don't know."

"Are you going to tell me what's going on?"

Nancy stood, but Bob didn't reply.

Finally she said, "I hope you're okay. You ping me when you're ready to talk?"

He could have asked her to stay, but didn't try to stop her primary subjective from leaving. Her form dematerialized. Was it the synthetic space projection? He replayed the scene. No. Her identity tags matched her projection as being her identity format. It was her, but not her. A different version? But how? And different how?

"Who the hell are you?"

The thing inside of him, the splinter of consciousness struggling to get free, had overcome him in his distraction. He was shoved out of his body, his virtual viewpoint pushed ten feet away. He stared back into his own face, a scowl of anger staring back at him.

"Who are you?" his body demanded.

And then he realized: That is not me. That was not *her*, and that is not me. That is not *my* body.

The memories rushed again into his external cognition systems, of lives long dead. Of his own lives. Bob steadied himself, looked into his own eyes, and noticed that they were different.

"Call me Shadow," he said quietly to himself.

8

"The cessation of suffering is attainable . . ."

The words floated to Bob through a steaming jungle, and he followed them into a clearing where he found a herd of massive dorsal-finned creatures. Halfway through mouthfuls of fern and bush, they swung their heads to observe him. A hooded figure walked past the animals and whispered, "Follow me."

Bob obeyed.

A hot sun burned high in the clear sky between the leaves, but not just one sun—a smaller bright pinpoint blazed beside and to the right of it. Two suns. Bob held one hand up to shield his eyes. Three fingers webbed with translucent green skin. He spread the webbing apart, and the fingers writhed and morphed into a single tentacle. The landscape, the animals, the vegetation—an alien world.

He inhabited an alien body—inhabited an *infected* alien mind.

Still he followed the hooded figure into the darkness of the forest underbrush. He had no agency, no way to stop what was happening. This event had already happened, was already congealed in the amber of time—a memory cleaved from deep inside himself, of a battle from far in the past. The Earth he knew was hundreds of light-years distant and was not yet even the Earth. Not the one he knew. At this slide along the universal timescale, the Earth he knew was still a primordial soup, the evolution of its version of life just beginning.

But not really beginning.

For the start of that life was a seed from beyond, a fragment of self-organizing genetic code thrown into the seas of space. The organic molecules floated on debris between stars, and with each habitable world this dust of life settled on, water combined with the heat energy of the nearest star and restarted the anti-entropic reaction. And not just water solvents. On frigid worlds there arose ammonia-based life, even methane-based. Again and again, on countless worlds, life evolved. Eyes. Stomachs. Teeth. Different but the same. Evolutionary pressures forced convergent solutions, the outward pressure of life against the inward pressure of entropy.

In the blink of an eye, ten millennia before, this race of green-hued creatures had evolved beyond farming. Two hundred years ago, they'd discovered radio waves. In the past ten years, they'd created their own nervenet technology, the ability to create sensory-realistic virtual worlds. The ability for the mind to transport itself beyond biological borders.

Made it possible for the infection to begin.

For not only genetic fragments of life code were floating between the stars, but information coded in electromagnetic waves, in neutrino and graviton waves. In everything. The universe was literally alive.

Bob inspected his green, webbed fingers in the light of the double sun.

Alive.

But with what?

"All is lost!" screamed Hezekiah. "And because of what? This boy?" He pointed an accusing finger at Bob.

Isaiah placed himself in front of the boy. "You are the King of Judah. You cast out the false idols. Yahweh will protect us."

The scroll of papyrus balanced on Bob's knees shook. He wasn't controlling this body, but only joyriding within it to get a view of the inside of the palace. Night was falling, and the smoke from the cooking fires of the two hundred thousand Assyrian troops camping outside the walls of Jerusalem drifted in, even here into the royal palace.

"Where is this *new* god you speak of?" Hezekiah scowled. "Isaiah, you had me smash the idols, destroy the temples."

Whenever humans were trapped, they always ran to the god-shaped hole in their heads. The thought burned the traces of Bob's mind in this world. "You want to see God?" he spat out between the teeth of the youth whose body he had stolen.

Hezekiah ignored him and glowered at Isaiah. "My father, Ahaz, has been murdered. Samaria is gone. We are trapped in this stinking hole of Jerusalem." He grabbed a smoldering pan of incense and threw it against the wall. The slaves cowered. "The twenty-four cities of Judah have been sacked. And you tell me now it was on this boy's words that you counseled me not to pay tribute to Sennacherib!"

"He will come," Bob heard himself saying. He leaned forward to look the king in the eye. "We will lay waste to the legions. I promise you."

"Your head will be the first thing I will present to Sennacherib come first light," growled Hezekiah.

But already there were the screams, of life being ripped from thousands of souls beyond the walls. Hezekiah's head turned, and he looked through billowing curtains into the screeching night. His scowl turned from one of anger to bewilderment.

And then to fear.

Bob flitted his conscious viewpoint out of the boy's body, up over the walls to swoop through the Assyrian encampment. The soldiers had drunk the water flowing from the cisterns, deep wells from below Jerusalem. Water that Bob had laced with a variant of nervenet technology, that had now infected the Assyrian troops. One by one, he snapped closed the information flowing through their nervous systems into their brains. These weren't conscious entities, he reasoned, but automatons, barely self-aware.

Why was Bob remembering this?

What was the importance?

And then the answer: This was the middle of another battle that was thousands of years in the making, a voice in his head replied. The survival of Jerusalem would enable the rise of Judaism, of Christianity, of Islam, and precipitate the rise of all Western and near-Eastern civilizations and ultimately the creation of America and Atopia.

It was an important nodal point in this history.

A critical juncture in the connectome of possible futures.

One he had to protect.

"Why do they always build fancy stuff to look like it's old Greek?" Sidgangster leaned back on the hood of their cherry-red GTO, propped himself up against the windshield, and stretched out his bare feet. He pulled his baseball cap lower over the red kerchief.

The dome of the Griffith Observatory loomed over the glitter of downtown Los Angeles, the luminous skyscrapers pillars of neon in a sea of twinkling lights that rolled in refracted atmospheric waves as the heat of the day dissipated into the night sky. The first brave stars punctured the indigo haze over the cityscape. At each side of the main dome of the observatory, two smaller domes joined it over a white stone structure, and warm yellow light bled out in squares onto the grass courtyard where oak and sycamore trees lined the road leading down out of the Hollywood hills.

Sid was right, the building could have been lifted straight from ancient Greece.

Bob remembered it clearly.

"It's a classic form," Bob replied. "Greek stuff is the best. Did you study Plato?"

He adjusted the body of the 1986-era gangster he was inhabiting, pushed it up on the windshield next to Sid. His gameworld mother was probably waiting on him in Compton, his character's memory informed him. He should feel guilty, *did* feel guilty—but it was too dangerous to go back into the city. They'd just injured two LAPD officers on their way out. He didn't feel guilty about that, though. It was the thought of his character's mother waiting by a cold meatloaf that inspired the emotion. They'd just finished a round of *Grand Theft* in this Los Angeles gameworld. It was time to reset. Bob felt the cold metal of the gun, smelled the sweaty tang of it in his hand as he wiped his face.

Sid-gangster's face crinkled, and his lips pulled back to expose two gold-capped front teeth. "So you've been there? Met Plato? Been to Greece? That's what you're saying?"

Beyond the luminous haze, a glittering high-density security blanket hugged this world tight.

"A version of me," Bob replied. Memories of Judah and Hezekiah, the battle with the Assyrians, jostled his memory.

"And what's in that POND data, this neutrino detector that Patricia built, you're in that too?"

"Other versions of me."

"How many versions of you are there, homie?" Sid-gangster's teeth glittered in the gathering gloom.

"Not exactly versions. Iterations. There's only one *me*, just more spread out. Like a wave function. I only resolve to a single point when I decide to look, if that makes any sense."

Sid-gangster pulled hard on both earlobes and sat up straighter. "And you're up there, too? All spread out?" He pointed at the pinpoints of stars appearing overhead.

"Cosmic microwave background radiation. My memories are encoded within it, and in neutrino waves from the creation of this universe. Once the initial conditions are set, I can control the dispersion in the early stages of the universe, before inflation begins."

"Wait a minute. *You* can? I thought it was this Destroyer you are chasing."

"I'm not chasing him. I've been forced into this."

"You know how crazy this sounds?" He paused and shrugged. "Or maybe how cool?"

"You've said the same thing—"

"A million times before. You said that already. That we've had this same conversation a million times before."

Bob nodded emphatically. "And you've agreed to help every time."

"Doesn't seem like it's worked out well so far." Sid-gangster shook his head. "I don't know, man."

Crickets chirped in the silence. Bob turned from looking at Sid to inspect the thicket of beavertail cacti beside the car, flowering in bright red bursts on top. Their GTO was parked just below Cahuenga Peak, the iconic letters of Hollywood visible to their right. A gray fox trotted between the cacti fronds and stopped to assess them. Wan yellow orbs of light reflected in its eyes. The fox looked real. Everything looked and smelled and tasted real. He wondered what this fox was thinking. Was it thinking what real foxes thought? Was it thinking *anything* at all? Did it know it wasn't real?

It didn't seem to think much of Bob and trotted off.

"A million?" Sid-gangster said to break the silence.

"I don't have a number for infinity." Bob couldn't do this by himself. He needed his master strategist. In all the times this had happened before, though, Sid had never given him voluntary access to his most private systems.

"Root pssi control is like handing your soul over." Sid-gangster shifted himself again.

"We need a new approach."

"I'm not sure about this *we* stuff. This isn't real, Bob. Somebody's messing with you. You know that, right?"

Somebody was *definitely* messing with him. "Then help me. I'm begging you." And he was.

His friend closed his eyes and pulled his baseball cap even lower. "So you're saying the development of nervenet technology is something that happens everywhere? Everywhere out there?" He pointed again at the sky, his eyes still closed.

"Convergent evolution. Just like the eye develops over and over again independently. It's a critical sensing apparatus. When intelligent species move from genetic to memetic evolution, the same things happen over and over again. Conscious minds move from the biological platforms they evolved on to computational substrates and then multiply. They always begin to simulate endless digital worlds."

"That overlap with physical worlds."

"Parallel universes."

"Frightening." Sid-gangster took a deep breath and exhaled slowly. "But not surprising."

"You don't need to tell me."

"And this thing you're chasing—"

"It's always one step ahead. Our world, everything in it is destroyed. Everyone here dies. All of our friends, all of our family. This world rarely progresses beyond this time. And if it doesn't end one way, it ends another. All the disasters that Patricia foresaw in her simulations, the reason why she's rushing to release her technology. It's all driven by this same entity." A pause. "I think."

"You expect me to help with some alien invader?"

"It's not alien. It's from here. It's someone—or some*thing*—from our world that escaped into the outside."

"And went *back* in time."

"Not back. Forward. Sideways. Somewhere in another universe."

"Another universe, huh? *Literally* another universe?"

Bob paused at that and inspected the cacti surrounding the car again, noticed the fractal pattern of their distribution across the arid sandy ground. "Have you ever noticed, the more that we learn about the universe, the more it seems to be governed by simple mathematical formulas? When we create simulated worlds, we use simple math rules to govern the basis of its creation."

"The same as the real world."

"But is it really a *real* world? Look at the quantum equations governing quarks and electrons. We get the same error-correcting codes that make our own communications networks operate. Why are these appearing in equations about supersymmetry and basic fundamental laws of the physical universe we live in?"

"It is weird, I'll give you that." Sid pursed his lips together, his bushy black eyebrows knitting together at the same time in something between a scowl and a grimace at the sourest thing he'd ever tasted. "So I'm someone in this other universe to you? Not the original Sid. Not *your* Sid?"

"Similar, but not quite."

"So what's the difference?"

"The difference is that someone from *here* destroys everything up *there*." Bob pointed at the same stars Sid had waved a hand at. "And I can't keep this world from being created. He's trying to prevent me from bringing us back here."

"He?"

"She. It. I don't know. All I know is that I want to come home. I want this to stop."

"This is messed up, and I'm *used* to being messed up with you, but this . . . this is trippy. This isn't what you think it is. *Can't* be what you think it is."

"You've already pointed that out."

Sid-gangster smoothed down his jeans and inspected a blood spatter, then tucked his hands below his elbows and stared intently into the haze over the city. He unclasped his hands from his elbows and brought them behind his head, a wide grin erupting on his face, exposing the gold-capped teeth again. "But this does sound like probably the greatest adventure of all time."

Details of log-in and override for Sid's internal systems arrived in Bob's inbox.

"You sure?" Bob asked.

"As sure as I am of anything, my friend, but let's give it a try."

Bob clicked the links, and nothing physical happened, but a warmth spread across his mind.

"You like being inside me?" Sid couldn't resist.

His friend was now a part of him, their neural systems fused. Bob released the rest of his information, details of the last world he could remember the fight happening in: of another version of him hiding the details of the Destroyer in Willy's body, of the fake hurricanes unleashed by Terra Nova, of Patricia collaborating with Mikhail Butorin—Sintil8—and his cult, of the collaboration with the Glasscutter hacking guilds, of the mysterious dark crystals discovered under cities, and of the competing nervenet technology.

And of Bob dying, of his life ending.

A part of Bob destroyed that universe.

"It's not your fault," Sid said, his voice just a digital whisper deep inside Bob's head.

They'd abandoned the Los Angeles simulation and hung in dimensionless gray space.

"So these crystals came from an alien race?"

"They first formed deep in Earth's history, floated in on interstellar dust, encrusted in the first land formations. The cratons. The only land masses that existed before plate tectonics began to reshape the Earth's surface."

"There's a craton under New York, and one under North Africa near Egypt," Sid said. "One under Papua New Guinea."

"The Yupno. They had no sensation of time." The mysterious head-hunter tribe high in the mountains, where Willy had gone to hide, the place that Vince had traced as a source of his future deaths.

"Makes sense."

"Of a weird sort."

"I can tell you one thing from all this," Sid said, his mind assimilating more and more. "This looks like a game, but on a grand scale. The biggest of games."

"And?"

"You and I are the masters of the gameworlds, right?" He forwarded Bob a plan, an outline of how to start. "We need to reset the game if we're going to do this."

"Of course," Bob replied.

Back in the Los Angeles gameworld, Bob raised his pistol, smiled at Sid-gangster, then pulled the trigger. Sid's head exploded in a burst of red mist. Bob put the barrel in his mouth and pulled again.

And he fell backward, through dimensionless black space.

The outlines of palm trees appeared.

"So what's the plan?" Sid asked, sitting in board shorts and holding a beer.

Bob picked up a gun.

"Jesus Christ, Bob, what are you doing?"

"We need to reset."

Bob pointed the gun at Sid and pulled the trigger, then put it in his own mouth and did the same.

9

The eagle coasted on a thermal, rising from the hot rock face below. It circled high into the sky as it peered below, hungry—starving in fact—but the raptor ignored the little creatures scurrying between the oleander bushes and fig and pomegranate trees. Its journey north from the verdant fields of Egypt, where the manmade mountains rose from the Nile, had taken weeks, guided by tenuous magnetic field lines that pulled it over the coast of Judah and mountains of Ararat and into the town of Ephesus, and then back out over the Aegean Sea.

Far below, a rise of dust. A figure walked along a path.

The bird of prey angled its feathers into the headwind. It soared upward in a sweeping angle that brought it around to dive at the ground. The urge inside that drove it forward had found its target. A wiry old man ambled into a rock-strewn gully dotted with ironwood and olive trees. The eagle stretched its wings back, the man unaware, and spread them wide in a fluttering wall of feathers to grab the man's arm as he reached for a boulder to steady himself. The eagle tensed its talons, dug them through the man's papery skin, and dug its beak into his chest before it released.

The man shrieked, his wail high and thin, and recoiled, sprawled into the dirt. The eagle squawked in response and settled into the sand, spread its wings wide before him, an avenging angel from the sky. The old man scurried on all fours back against a pile of rocks, his eyes wide and lips pulled back in a terrified grimace exposing a mouthful of broken teeth. He rubbed the wound on his chest, slick with not just his own blood but also the eagle's. The bird cocked its head to one side and inspected the emaciated Jew. He was naked save for a black turban atop his head and a matching thong wrapped around his torso. Bushy gray eyebrows above deep-set brown eyes, a wild mustache curled up at the edges almost to the gray hair that sprouted out from his eyes. His cheeks and chin were roughly shaved. He stank, even to the eagle's limited olfactory senses.

"What do you want, devil?" the man yelled.

The eagle sidestepped in the dirt and cocked its head to the other side.

"We have met before," the entity inside the raptor replied, its voice an echo inside the man's head. "In the Western Deserts, where I gave you the visions you craved, the prophecies for which you were banished to these islands." The eagle pressed forward, and the man retreated into a cave hollowed out in the hill beside the path.

"Who are you?" the man whispered. "*What* are you?"

The question triggered a cascade. A blossom of awareness grew from the pinpoint of a splinter wedged in the primitive mind of the raptor. The nanoscale particles flowing through its bloodstream congealed into a mass in its gut, rewiring its neural network. A flood of memories coursed into the growing awareness.

Who am I?

I am Bob.

The connection had been made, with some of the nanoscale particles transferred from the bird's blood into the old man's. The particles suffused through his bloodstream, in just seconds filtered through the blood-brain barrier, and burrowed through neuron-myelin sheaths into the core of his unprotected mind's circuitry. The old man's eyes widened into saucers as his mind's eye was snatched away, the outlines of the shadows on the cave wall replaced by the billowing wall of flame of the Atopian slingshot test over the waters of the Pacific.

"A battle is being waged in heaven between the forces of light and dark," Bob said to the old man. "I am here to show you the truth, to lift the veil." He let the image of the fireball fade and replaced this with images of a world he once knew, of great empty ships plying the endless seas, of skies filled with drones, of masses of humanity crammed into cities of skyscrapers.

Terror echoed from one corner to the other in the old man's mind. "I don't understand."

Bob had begun speaking in Aramaic to the old man, but he shifted into old Greek. "This is the end of time I am showing you," he explained. He let the images scroll forward through his memories, his own personal memories: the walk across the desert with the priest, to the supercollider in Africa and the impulse that fractured that universe. "This is the truth of this world, this is what I am uncovering for you. I will be there at the end, and at the beginning. I will die, but will be reborn, to be here with you."

Bob planted their viewpoint into the ridge of mountains in Montana, where the Reverend's Commune stood, when Vince had journeyed here. A replay of a memory. He pointed into the sky. "The sign will be the star with two tails." The comet Wormwood splayed out in the sky across the stars. "And three riders that signal the uncovering of the truth." He filled the old man's mind with an image of the head of Allied Command, and of Jimmy, and of himself, the tattered, emaciated image of him emerging from the slums of Lagos.

"Three men, do you understand, John?" Bob towered over the man back in the cave in the hills over Patmos. "Three."

The old man, John of Patmos, shoved his frail body into a tiny corner of the cave. "Are you God?"

"I am the son of a man, just as you."

"But you come back from the dead?"

"There is no death."

"What do you want from me?"

"Three."

"I heard that you talked to Patricia Killiam." Bob's father pointed his butter knife at his son, let it waggle in the air a few times before returning to his toast.

"I guess I did." Bob rubbed the back of his neck with one hand, his memories fuzzy of the day before. The slingshot test. The bright burning in the sky. That was just now, wasn't it? Something was wrong in his head. For the thousandth time, he promised he would stop with the drugs. Enough was enough. A half memory of a dream, of an old man in a desert—not a desert, an island. And where was Sid? They'd been playing a game. He'd killed Sid, and that was normal enough in the gameworlds, but usually he did it by accident. Why did he do it on purpose?

And why had he talked to Patricia?

Tidbits of information escaped him.

Gotta stop with the drugs, man.

A seagull squawked in the distance, joined in a chorus with its friends. Bob was having breakfast with his family on the rooftop deck of their habitat, a family luxury granted to the Baxters because of Bob's father's senior role as PR director for Cognix Corporation. His mother and father sat to the left and right of him, and a virtual projection of Martin, Bob's dead brother, sat directly in front of Bob, a floppy mop of blond hair over his clueless digital blue eyes.

Jimmy Scadden, Bob's adopted brother, swept into the room from the stairs leading up. "Conscious transference, that's quite a jump from surfing." He worked at the Solomon House research center.

He'd obviously talked with Patricia. "And the Pacific Ocean Neutrino Detector? What do you want with that?"

"Patricia took me back quick." Bob honestly didn't know why he'd asked to get involved. "Must need new talent."

"Talent?" Jimmy smiled a condescending grin and bit into an apple. "That's what you call what you do?"

"And what do you call what you do?"

"Work."

"And that's the problem, right there."

"That I work?"

"If you love it, shouldn't *be* work."

Jimmy snorted. "I love my work, you can bet on that." He bit into the apple again. "Dad, Martin, are you guys ready to go?"

It was Martin's birthday, and Jimmy had organized a field trip to show off some of his research. Of course their father was proud. He seemed more proud of Jimmy, their adopted son, than their *real* boys, Bob and Martin. The thought was an annoying itch in the back of Bob's mind, one that he couldn't quite seem to scratch.

"See all of you later." Bob's dad put his napkin down, smiled to everyone around the table to register an appropriate level of politeness, and this done, he flitted his primary subjective off to the Solomon House. His body remained—under the control of his proxxi—still smiling vacantly. It began the job of clearing the table.

Martin rolled his eyes, but carefully so that only Bob would see. "I better go."

Bob nodded, and Martin flitted off to follow his father. They shared disdain for Jimmy, one of the few reasons Bob was happy to put up with the ruse of this synthetic space projection of his dead brother. That, plus it made his mother happy.

"Honey, are you okay?" she asked. She leaned forward to put her hand on his.

"I'm fine," Bob replied. It was an expression that always meant the opposite, and using it always elicited the same response.

"What's wrong?" His mother's eyes glistened, as they did when she wanted to reach inside her child's mind to pry out something hurtful, something that could tear a wound, a bent nail in a board that might trip him up. His father was the one who hammered them back in. Beyond her blue eyes, waves on the seas reflected the sun, lighting her frizzy blonde hair in a halo around her intent face. "You can tell me, whatever it is," she whispered and gripped his arm tighter.

Did he love her? Did Bob *love* his mother? She loved him. That much he was certain, and despite his father's nail-hammering habits, he loved Bob, too. He saw it in their eyes, and he loved them in return, but the love didn't feel genuine, somehow. Had never felt genuine. A view of love through a frosted pane of glass.

Perhaps that was the source of his self-loathing. Maybe it wasn't just his brother's suicide, the pain and guilt he hid beneath. Maybe it was just an excuse. Some part of him felt he wasn't worthy, wasn't really a part of this family, and that was why having Jimmy come into the family drove Bob away that much further. Why he felt like they loved him more. Why he felt like they *should*.

"Nothing is wrong," Bob said after a pause.

"Talk to me," his mother persisted.

He didn't feel the same love for his own mother that he did for Nancy. Of course, his love for his old girlfriend felt more like an obsession, a man hanging on to a life raft. Maybe that was another reason he kept her away. He didn't like feeling desperate, didn't like the feeling of *needing* thousands of dimstim fans, the simultaneous need to push everyone close to him away. Everyone except Sid. And speaking of Sid, where was he today? Bob queried his proxxi, but his data feeds were blank. Maybe his dad had Jimmy cut him off. Not funny.

"Maybe you should come to church with me," added his mother.

That was the wrong thing to say, and she knew it. Why did she keep bringing it up? Why did people have these god-shaped holes that appeared in their heads whenever there was a problem? The man behind his mother, dressed in a toga and sandals—until this moment staring out at the ocean—got to his feet.

"Not a word from you," Bob spat. He pointed an accusing finger at the demure bearded man and got up from the table. He'd had enough of breakfast, and wasn't in a mood for this. He had to find Sid. Something was wrong.

His mother's personal Jesus, he couldn't stand him. Her Jesus followed her around everywhere, yet another absurd manifestation made possible by the wonders of the limitless virtual reality. At least, absurd to Bob. His mother talked to Jesus more than she talked to anyone else, and at times like this, she often used Jesus to talk for her.

"Please, Bob, I asked him to talk to you. Sid told me to get him to talk to you."

"Sid?"

"Sid is a member of our church," Jesus pointed out, pulling out the chair Martin had been sitting on. He sat down to join them at the table.

Bob sat back down himself, deflated and confused. "Where is Sid?" He still couldn't find his friend anywhere in his informational networks.

The Elèutheros began as a Catholic sect convinced that there were strong affinities between Christianity, the philosophy of free and open source software, and the adoption of open formats and protocols. The ultimate nerds of the Vatican. It grew over time, and when Atopia was founded, the sect gained a foothold, a bulwark against the decay of moral fabric encouraged by limitless virtual reality. Bob knew Sid was a member, was a part of their hacking collective. Just doing the work of God, Sid liked to joke when Bob needled him about it.

"What do you imagine God to be?" Jesus asked.

Bob gritted his teeth and exhaled long and slow enough to let his mother know what he thought of this kidnapping. He felt his mother's eyes on him and relented. "I don't imagine there is some bearded old benevolent grandfather—*your father*—sitting in the clouds somewhere and looking down on us, if that's what you mean."

"I am merely a metaphor," said Jesus. "This form before you is a convenience, not a literal interpretation. I am here because your mother likes to interact with me like this. Surely you can understand."

"I guess."

Jesus's eyes narrowed. He steepled his fingers atop an imaginary church. "The Church of Elèutheros imagines God as more of a hacker, in the original sense of a tinkerer with code."

"So he's still an old man, just sitting shirtless in a darkened room, bent over a keyboard?"

"He created Adam in the beginning so that man would love him. He created man in his image; therefore, God is also in our image. Do you see?"

Bob sighed again, but only on the inside. Gobbledygook. "So we're all God? Isn't that pagan?"

"There is God in all of us, yes." Jesus smiled at his mother, and they both nodded. "And he created us to love him and therefore love ourselves. Do you see?"

"*Jesus*," Bob cursed under his breath. How did he let himself get trapped here?

"Yes?" the personal deity replied.

"Not you."

"He means, you need to love yourself first." His mother still had hold of his arm, and she gripped so tight it felt as if it caused the tears to well in her eyes. "Love yourself," she repeated. "That's what he means."

Love yourself. That's what Nancy had said to him, too. Thinking of her tied a knot in Bob's stomach.

"Check it out," said a new voice.

Bob was busy staring at the floor, trying to look anywhere but at Jesus and his mother. He looked up to his right. Sid had appeared at the table, a virtual projection glittering inside a private security blanket, but not just any security blanket. This was something new—something *hard*—and he wasn't outside. Somehow he was *inside* Bob's cognition framework.

"Where have you been?" Bob asked his friend on a secured private channel. Neither his mother nor Jesus perceived Sid among them.

"Ask him about the Horsemen of the Apocalypse," Sid said.

"Apocalypse?"

"Just do it."

Bob blinked, his mind processing, and turned back to Jesus. "Tell me about the Horsemen of the Apocalypse."

It was Jesus's turn to blink. "The Three Horsemen?"

"See?" Sid turned to a shadow sitting behind him in the virtual cave. "Three."

"Three?" Bob asked. He was confused. What was the significance? There had already been three.

Sid nodded to the shadow behind him. "We changed history," he said, but wasn't talking to Bob. "Not four Horsemen anymore. Only three here."

"That doesn't make sense," said the shadowy figure behind Sid. "We changed all that," it said, "but we're still here?"

"Convergence, like you said," Sid said to the figure. "Atopia is the fulcrum."

"Who are you talking to?" Bob shrugged an apology to his mother and Jesus and pulled his primary subjective away from the breakfast table and into a private meeting space that he enveloped around Sid.

"Getting trapped inside a loop of time, replaying to stop destruction," Sid said, forwarding an information packet to Bob to explain who the shadow figure was. "Doesn't that sound familiar? Nodal points in time that change the future, that's what you're describing, moving the timeline around. Sound familiar? How much do you really know about Vince?"

10

Flickers of oily fire reflected on dark waters. Bonfire flames burned high, and the revelers and religionists and penitent writhed together on soggy patches of ground dotted along the edges of old Lake Pontchartrain. Wayfarers' boats lit up garish reds and greens against the white halo of New Orleans hung back on the horizon. The first stars of the night appeared through the smoke-filled haze amid the crackle of firecrackers and strains of jazz. The celebration of Saint John of the Apocalypse had just begun.

Awaking from a dream into a dream was the only way Bob could describe it.

He'd never liked going to sleep as a child. It didn't mark just the end of a day, but the end of everyone who had lived that day. There was no guarantee of waking up again, and those who did weren't really the same people. New people awoke, their minds subtly altered—the same memories but processed differently—into a new and different world. He felt this now, leaving one universe and traveling to the next, awaking from a dream into a mind both new and old.

Into a universe both old and new.

At first, there was just a sense of place, of watching something happen—and then, a rush of breath, but without the breathing. An inflation of awareness that brought the questions: Where am I? What is this place? *Who* am I? Bob's meta-cognition frameworks bootstrapped themselves, and his consciousness blossomed forth from the nether-worlds, from the deep sleeps of forever. It awoke hungry, consuming huge gulps of information about the framework of existence it found itself within.

Tiny splinters of his psyche waited, mindless, like the old software daemons running in ancient mainframes, pieces of code that ran automatically in the background. The daemons watched for an exact sequence of events, a pattern match in time and space, and when the key fit, the combination was unlocked, gears opened within gears to unfold ever-increasing layers of complexity.

Bob's daemons were everywhere and watched everything.

His daemons waited for the moment to summon him and bring him back to life.

He wasn't quite awake yet. His awareness was still confined to the tiny bee-drone his daemons had selected as the optimal shell to carry his embryonic mind. The drone's sensors fixed on noise in the distance. An open aluminum boat with an outboard combustion engine, a withered old man attached to and directing it. In the middle of the boat, another old man held aloft a bottle. Of alcohol. He took a swig and wiped his mouth with the back of one hand. The face was familiar. The slight frame, the twitch of the cheek. Memories flooded Bob's networks.

It was Vincent Indigo.

His old friend.

The boat's engine cut, and it slid into the mud and grass at the coast of one of the half-submerged islands, a massive effigy of Saint John burning in its center, sparks and cinders tripping away and up into the black sky. A *mambo*—a voodoo priestess in flowing white robes—reached for and took Vince's hand as he disembarked. Hoodoo came out of Northern Africa, the same area of the craton, the most primeval of Earth's rock, where the Egyptian pyramids had arisen, where the crystal mountains in the White Desert grew through the sands. The same place that Bob had journeyed through with the priest, the Destroyer, the entity that was chasing him.

Bob's mind was reassembling more and more of itself. He'd set his daemons to awake him at this moment, just before the Alliance forces would attack, the fury of which would create a blank spot in the local wikiworld feed. He had to keep invisible. The other version of himself in this world was in the desert right now with the priest. Coming any closer would alert it to his presence, would terminate this world before he had a chance to get what he needed.

The bee-drone circled, dropped down toward the *houngans*, the male voodoo priests, and dancers twisting in a prayer circle around the burning effigy. He tensed the drone's abdomen, readied the needle of its injector. It was a drug-delivery drone, already spiked with a load of off-label smarticles to deliver into a victim's bloodstream. His daemons had commandeered it from a local drug pusher. Bob-drone circled around and around, buzzed past Vince's head once, then delivered the dose by stabbing the drone's needle into his neck. His old friend was too entranced by the ceremony to notice and simply swatted at his neck.

Vince's automated defenses, the networks extending into the future and past by his proxxi, Hotstuff, were almost impenetrable. Attempting to breach his temporal shell using a purely informational attack was risky, so Bob's daemons had concocted a plan to bypass with a physical attack. Direct injection. The load of infected smarticles diffused fast, and Bob co-opted his friend's internal networks. His mind infused with Vince's, faster than Hotstuff could defend. She tried to warn Vince at the final instant—but it was too late, and Bob wasn't a threat. He wasn't going to hurt Vince. He just needed to talk to him.

Allied forces had already breached the perimeter.

From the image of the fire dancing in Vince's optics, Bob pressed himself into his friend's awareness. His presence expanded into a dark figure that loomed over and around the bonfire's flames. The houngans seemed able to see him. Vince's eyes grew wide. "Bob?" he said, his mouth agape. "Are you okay? We lost you in New York. Where are you? What happened?"

"Everything's okay," Bob whispered soothingly into his friend's mind.

Vince still thought that this instance of Bob was the same as the one wandering now in the desert. It would be too confusing, in the short time they had, to explain otherwise. An explosion lit up the swampland to the south, its flames roiling up into the darkness. A military mechanoid loomed from the moss-covered oaks a hundred yards away. An eagle-drone swooped down to snatch Vince in its talons. It was one of Mikhail Butorin's drones, part of the Aesthetic arsenal, rescuing Vince from the Allied attack. At the same time, Vince's mind was carried away into the virtual private world of Butorin, the log cabin high amid dark forests that rolled through the foothills of the Ural Mountains.

Bob took a backseat in Vince's mind. He knew Vince had this meeting with Butorin and wanted to experience it, gather more information. If anything personified evil, Mikhail Butorin was it, yet Patricia had allied herself with him before she died and let his spies into Atopia. She had told Vince and Bob that they had to meet the gangster. Why? It still wasn't clear. Bob listened to Vince and Butorin. The old gangster described fighting with the Red Army against the Nazis, the German High Command's obsession with the occult and an early Buddhist statue carved from a meteorite. He said that Willy's body had something inside it he'd been looking for. Bob watched the Russian hand Vince copies of Christian-era manuscripts he had dug up in the deserts of Egypt. The meeting in the virtual world finished quickly, and the eagle-drone deposited Vince into a knee-deep swamp a few hundred yards from Agent Sheila Connors.

Bob materialized in synthetic space form beside him.

"Is Sid with you?" Vince asked after decrypting Bob's metatags.

The question surprised Bob. He always carried a version of Sid with him now, ever since Sid had let him make a full copy. He tried to wake his friend—his sidekick—up whenever he could and update him, and Sid wouldn't have it any other way. Vince didn't mean that, though; he meant the instance of Sid in this world, and *that* Sid was with the Underminers.

"Sid is safe. He's still in New York," Bob replied after what seemed an eternity of cycles, but little more than a millisecond later. "But I have some questions. How deep into the Atopian infrastructure is Phuture News wired?"

Was Bob stuck in a diagnostic loop? That was his big question in wanting to talk with Vince. Was Bob's awareness jumping into the past and forward into the future stuck in some corner of Vince's Phuture News simulation loop?

Something had happened, something that started on Atopia when Vince became stuck in his own time trap, created by Patricia and Kesselring. This wasn't the first time the three of them had fought. Back when Vince had started Phuture News, Kesselring had attempted to steal it, and Patricia had defended Vince, but at the cost of needing to side with Kesselring to start the Atopian project. Was there more to Vince being stuck in his death spiral?

Vince stood tall, his forehead creased. "On the deepest levels. The technologies evolved together, they're integral to each other—but you know that. What are you thinking?" He began to trudge through the muck toward Agent Connors.

"You created Phuture News as a way of predicting the future, so you wouldn't let a loved one die again."

It was a famous story—almost as famous as Vince himself—of a night, decades before, when a terrorist cyberattack had derailed a Boston-to-New-York commuter train, killing his fiancée. It had been the start of his obsession with predicting the future.

"In a way, or at least, that was my initial motivation. Now, I don't know . . ." His voice faded.

"Now you're using it to save yourself."

"Wouldn't you?" Vince pushed aside a carpet of moss hanging from a tree branch and suction-pulled his left foot from the swampy muck to advance another step.

"And if the whole world was threatened. What would you do then?"

Vince paused from struggling with the swamp to consider the question. "Anything, I suppose."

"Anything?"

"There is evil in the world. I've lived long enough to know that. And if I had the power to stop it, I'd stop at nothing. I'm not someone who goes half measures. What happened to you in New York?"

"Jimmy attacked us," Bob explained, following the storyline of this universe. "But that's not important right now." It was Bob's turn to pause and consider. "Do you really believe your phutures are real?"

"I just started the company. It's not like I *own*—"

"But you believe they're alternate physical realities that actually exist somewhere else? That entering them through sensory-realistic virtual reality is a portal into them?"

"I think so. In a way. And that's what the experts say."

"Don't you qualify as an expert?"

"Patricia was the one obsessed with phuturing," Vince replied. "You should ask her, but unfortunately"—he exhaled hard and bowed his head—"she's dead." He leaned against a tree branch and inspected the moss on it. "Hard to tell what's real or not, if you ask me."

Bob decided to try another tack. Maybe sharing some information? "This thing we're chasing, I think it came from Atopia. Escaped into the multiverse in the explosion of evolution when pssi was released."

"*Was* released? You mean it's from the future?"

Bob clucked. This version of Vince was stuck in a unidirectional timeline, despite the temporal immune system Vince had set up around himself that stretched into a future and past bubbling around him.

"It must be hard for you," Vince said in Bob's silence as they trudged forward through the swamp muck. "Being born on Atopia, I mean. It is too bad you didn't get to talk more with Patricia before she died."

Why did he keep on saying Bob should have talked to Patricia more? He added her to the list of dead people he had to interrogate, by reversing through the stream of parallel universes.

But did she really die?

Was she the entity pulling the universes apart? Was she angry about something? Maybe upset about her biological self being killed? This was one more in a long list of questions Bob was trying to answer. She died in this timeline, but did some part of her escape? She was trying to control the future—just like Vince, but on a grander scale—and was willing to sacrifice almost everything about humanity to save a small part of it. She had more than a small element of megalomania to her, and more than that of preachiness. If this thing had started in Atopia, then Patricia was the nodal point that defined its origin.

"Must be hard to know what's real or not for you," Vince added, and shrugged in an uncommitted way. "But what difference would it make? I've always wondered why our best theories of physical reality say it only really materializes when we look at it. When we're not paying attention, the microscopic world of quantum physics is fuzzy and undecided. Exactly what you'd expect to see if we *were* living in a simulation, right?" Vince laughed at that.

"You think it's funny?"

"In an ironic kind of way. One thing I would say . . ."

Bob waited.

The corners of Vince's mouth edged into a conspiratorial grin. "I hope we *are* living in a simulation. That we're all simulated."

The thought tied Bob's mind into knots of revulsion. The one thing he wanted more than anything was to get out of the endless pit he'd been cast into, to find a way to get home—back into his own skin—with no threat of the Destroyer looming over him. "Why do you say that?"

"Because everyone behaves themselves better if they think someone is watching. Basic human psychology. We tend to act badly if we think nobody will know, but we behave on a much higher moral plane if we think someone will see what we're doing. So if it's a simulation we're in, the big question is, who's watching? And how will they judge us?" He laughed again. "Better do good things, my friend."

Who was watching? Bob hadn't thought of it like that. "And who created it?" he whispered.

"Endless parallel universes, simulated universes—in the end I think it's all the same thing," Vince added. "Infinity and infinity overlap at some point, isn't that what you always said?"

"I was trying to be clever."

"So be clever then."

Up ahead, the trees cleared. They could just see Agent Connors in the distance.

"You know who you should go talk to?" Vince said. "The Reverend, Willy's uncle in the Commune. When Willy's body got there, it was looking up all the old apocalyptic texts, and that seems to be what Butorin is obsessed with as well. Maybe this end-of-the-world cult stuff isn't as harmless as it seems. And he wouldn't let you in, remember? Just me and Brigitte. He wouldn't let you and Sid in, pushed you off to New York . . . and then that attack there." Vince's eyes settled on Agent Connors repairing the drone.

It did seem odd. Why hadn't the old Reverend let Bob in, especially after Bob had saved his niece from falling under that transport in the village?

"Vince, I'm going to have to take your memory of this talk," Bob said without explaining.

"Hey, what? What do you—"

But Bob had already yanked it out.

11

"How are we going to get inside?" Sid asked.

"Just wait." Bob's daemons had woken him for a reason, but he was exhausted. He'd just awakened Sid's mind as well. He needed help.

They were inhabiting a red fox that had gobbled up the hawk he used to fly to the outskirts of the Commune. The two of them—Bob and Sid—were just voices inside the fox's head, but of course it couldn't understand them. The remnants of the old machine Bob had infected in this world existed only in patches, around the primordial Gondwana and orogen cratons now distributed into Africa and America, so his daemons had to transport physically from these hot spots. The dark crystals were spreading in this world, but weren't everywhere yet.

The fox sat back on its haunches to give Sid and Bob a better view through its eyes.

Of the new apocalyptic cults that sprang up in the mid-twenty-first century, the Commune was the granddaddy of them all. The trees at the edge of the forest thinned on the plateau, and in the clearing was a depressed bowl in the earth two miles across, ringed by pine forests and backed by the mountains of Montana, their peaks capped in white. In the center sat the network of dusty roads, wooden buildings, and farmhouses that made up the Commune. The sun had set behind the mountain range, a gray pall thrown across the landscape. Clouds gathered over the snowy peaks, while brown-spotted cows huddled for protection under the wide branches of red-barked blackjacks that lined the edges of the row-cut farm fields.

A shimmering halo hung in the sky over it all, the mile-high defensive shield of aerial plankton, tiny bots that formed a shell a few dozen feet thick and attacked any unauthorized intruder. They wouldn't kill, but they would disable the neurological systems of any biological incursions. The shield also acted as a giant Faraday cage, protecting the Commune from outside electromagnetics across a spectrum from visual to microwave to radio. The Commune was neo-Luddite in faith, and inside the high-tech exterior, no technology more sophisticated than hammers and nails was permitted. Except for the Reverend—he had a data link in the church at the center of town, but it had the feeling of a trap, of a honeypot to attract errant digital bees. The Commune was purpose-built to keep outsiders away and almost impossible for Bob to worm his way inside for an informational attack.

They needed to be invited.

Sid used the fox's nose to sniff the air, propped it up onto its hind legs, and stretched out its paws. The fox's rich olfactory sense provided more sensory data than its visual channels, and the area seemed clear of threats. The distant clouds churned over the mountaintops, and in the center of the town, a puff of dust. A horse and cart began to wind its way toward them.

The fox's nose twitched. "Did you send someone to get us?" Sid asked.

"Sort of."

Sid sat the fox back down. "So do you think it's Vince?" He had a hard time being still in any form and started the fox pacing through the tall grass at the edge of the forest. He'd just assimilated the talk Bob had had with Vince in the swamps outside New Orleans.

Bob rubbed the fox's snout on a foreleg. "I don't know."

"He thinks phutures are real," Sid pointed out. "That alternate timelines are *real* parallel universes—and he collapses the ones he doesn't like. That don't suit him."

"The ones that kill him, you mean. And Patricia did the same thing, but worse."

"Patricia Killiam"—Sid shivered the tiny fox—"is a whole other ball of fur. She was doing it to save everyone, he was just doing it to save himself. And you were close to him. Maybe he's the one causing this. *And* he's got a lot of pain in him. He doused himself in as much booze as you used drugs. No wonder you guys were such good friends."

"I include you in that grouping."

"True." Sid turned the fox in tight circles. "But what did he say? He hoped that we were all simulations? For a guy that seems to think reality isn't real, he sure seems determined not to let himself die."

"That's just human nature."

"If humans are *natural* themselves," Sid clucked and giggled at his own joke. "And you let yourself be killed, sacrificed your physical body. You didn't run away into some other alternate future."

Now it was Bob's turn to shiver the fox's fur. Talking like this made his head hurt, and he tried not to remember that time, the start of his journey into the multiverse, when his physical body had died and he'd been cast out, uploaded his mind into the cloud. He'd hardly noticed a difference.

"So do you think he's your Destroyer?" Sid persisted. "Vince the Destroyer?"

"Maybe."

It was hard to say what escaped into the multiverse. This thread of consciousness outside the Commune was just one of dozens of others out investigating myriad strands of thought—assessing Rick Strong and the defensive networks on Atopia, many Atopians themselves, including the collective of the Hunter, the underling of Jimmy who had set off the neural bomb in New York. And Jimmy himself, of course. A part of Bob wanted to believe that Jimmy wasn't the one in control of himself, that something else was influencing him, but maybe that was the part of him that wanted to see the good in people.

The explosive power of the evolutionary chain that was set off when pssi was released into the world was hard to track. In an instant, billions of human minds and physical organisms had moved into the digital realm, memetics replacing genetics, reproducing themselves in almost endless virtual universes. The pace of evolution—once measured in decades and millennia—had shortened to seconds and milliseconds. Within weeks of the release, of society sliding into the posthuman era, the world had ended. That universe had been destroyed by something within it. The mysterious dark crystals they discovered, the ancient nervenet, were a technology Bob had coopted but wasn't in control of. It seemed to permeate everywhere and everything.

"We're still criminals in this world," Sid reminded Bob. "That reality-skin infection that almost destroyed Atopia, we were implicated. Maybe we should be investigating Tyrel and Terra Nova."

"We're going to get to that next."

Sid froze the fox in its tracks. "We're not going to have to restart again, are we?"

Bob had to rewind time again to get back to this moment.

He departed the stream of consciousness, talking to Vince to reenter another parallel universe at an earlier point in time. This time, though, the experience wasn't just like awaking from a dream. It felt more like drowning in molasses, stuck underground in the quicksands of time. He had to claw his way out to take a desperate breath of consciousness. The spawning of universes wasn't infinite; they were being cleaved away as he moved forward. His paths forward were becoming narrower. Something was trying to stop him—it knew he was here.

The claustrophobic fear of being trapped still tingled in Bob's metasenses, the sensory network that extended into the world around him, but also into the informational database of his accumulated past, gleaned from the cosmic background microwave radiation data and neutrino flow of the combined sensing devices of this planet. For he hadn't just existed on this world alone, but his consciousness had awoken on millions of other alien worlds that developed nervenet technology. In the back of his mind, images of strange plants, of massive, green dorsal-finned animals and webbed fingers on his hands. The battle he was waging extended everywhere, but always led back here, to this place.

To this world.

The coming storm clouds roiled over the mountaintops as the horse and buggy coming from the center of the Commune grew nearer. There was one driver, dressed in black with a matching wide-brimmed hat. The rolling clouds hit the Commune's aerial plankton perimeter, skidding across its surface to form a dome high in the sky.

Sid backed the fox up ten paces to the cover of low-hanging pine branches. "What's your plan, exactly? You're not going to let them shoot us, are you?" The experience of letting the hawk they'd originally inhabited be eaten by the fox had been traumatic for Sid. "You're not planning on having them *eat* us?"

In the sky, a keening whine.

"Relax," Bob said again. "Our ride is here."

A sleek electric turbofan skimmed the treetops. Its landing gear deployed as it circled and descended, the fox's fur blowing back. Leaves and twigs scattered. The transport settled onto the grass, its engine's whine cycling down. The cockpit opened and a young man stepped out—his hair close-cropped in a buzz cut, a friendly smile on his freckled face above a sturdy frame. It was their friend Willy, or at least, Willy's body. His mind was disconnected from it right now.

"How did you know . . . ?" Sid twitched the fox's nose again.

"Vince said Willy's body came to the Commune just before we got here, remember?"

The horse and cart rumbled over the dirt track leading to the edge of the perimeter. There wasn't just one person in the cart. There was a woman as well, with fair blonde hair. She waved at Willy.

Bob took control of the fox and darted out from under the pine. He zigged and zagged toward Willy, then lunged to bite his leg. The fox's fangs sank through his jeans, and he held on long enough for the fox's saliva—loaded with particles encoding Bob and Sid—to enter Willy's bloodstream. Their target yelped and kicked the fox away, but already Bob was in, his mind fusing with whatever was inside Willy's head.

"Hey, Bob," said Wally, Willy's proxxi, sensing their arrival—and not the least bit surprised.

It wasn't the first time Bob had inhabited Willy's body. They had switched bodies all the time when they were kids on Atopia. "Wally," Bob replied. "Mind if I take over?"

"Not at all." The proxxi melted into the background.

Bob used Willy's body to wave to the people on the arriving horse and cart. Willy's mother waved back again, more enthusiastically this time. Bob recognized her from Willy's accessible memories. The aerial plankton opened a path in the perimeter, and Bob walked through it. "Zephyr," he called out, "it's been a long time."

The boy driving the cart waved his wide-brimmed hat and hooted in return as he pulled up the horses in a cloud of dust. Willy's mother jumped from the cart and rushed to hold Bob in her arms.

The horse and cart and its three physical occupants trundled along the dirt path through the outskirts of the Commune. Willy's mother had her arm around Bob—in Willy's body—and he needed to maintain their cover. He had access to enough of Willy's memories to carry on a conversation, pretend he was Willy. They passed men dressed in black, women in frocks, a group of them raising the frame of a barn, and then turned onto a street of neat row houses of white-painted clapboard. The spire of the church rose up in the center.

Somehow, the whole place had been swept clean of the dark crystals that now grew outside.

A virtual projection of Sid materialized beside Zephyr, but only Bob could see or hear him.

"How did you contact Willy?" Sid asked.

"I didn't. I just knew he was coming here. Wally was trying to protect Willy, that's why he left Atopia. He had the POND data, knew that the Destroyer had infected Atopia. Tyrel and Butorin helped him escape."

"Wally didn't seem surprised when you suddenly showed up in his body," Sid pointed out.

"How many times—"

"I know, I know, we did it all the time," Sid conceded. "But when Butorin talked to Vince, he said that he helped Willy's body escape Atopia because there was something in Willy's body he'd been searching to find for a hundred years."

"And that's what I need your help with," Bob said. "Another reason I brought us here. Butorin helped him escape, but Wally hid from him as soon as he did. Why did he do that?"

"Is that a question?"

"Willy is fresh from Atopia," Bob continued. "Whatever Butorin wanted must still be inside. Can you root around in Willy's memories and data stores to see what's in here?"

"And what are you going to do?"

The horse and cart were just pulling past the church in the center of town, and Bob leaned forward to put a hand on Zephyr's arm. "Can you drop me off? I really need to speak with the Reverend."

The ruddy-faced boy smiled a toothy grin. "Of course, partner. That's a good idea." He pulled up on the reins.

"Is that okay?" Bob turned to Willy's mother. She nodded, her eyes still wet with tears. She hadn't seen her boy in years.

"And is that okay with you?" Bob asked Sid on their private channel. "Vince said Willy's body went into the church archives here to look at the collection of old texts. I'm going to go have a look myself."

The Commune was one of the wealthiest religious institutions on the planet. Its vault of rare books was kept under the humble wooden church, and the texts Bob wanted to look at were on display under glass. Incandescent bulbs cast warm yellow light, and the room smelled musty, of old books and humid earth.

He walked the lengths of the aisles, peered at the yellowed papers and fragments of scrolls written in Greek, Aramaic, and the more ancient scratches of Sanskrit. He could decipher them all and compared them against the data he'd already collected, against what he already knew: the Book of Daniel, of Joel and Zechariah, Baruch, and stories of Gog and Magog in the Hebrew texts. What had Wally been looking for?

"You are not my nephew."

The Reverend stood on the side staircase leading down into the crypts. Dressed in a simple black robe, his forehead was creased in angry furrows, his face flushed, his white mustache quivering. The yellow light reflected from the sweat on his bald scalp, a halo of white hair rimming large ears that protruded outward, the flat sledge of his nose between deep-set eyes.

Bob smiled his most defenseless grin. "Uncle, it is good to—"

"Do not play games with me." The Reverend stepped toward Bob and fixed him with his bushy-eyebrowed stare.

"How do you know?" Bob decided against further deception. This priest knew something he didn't.

"I know my nephew. Leave his body. Now."

"I can't do that."

"How did you get in here?"

"All this won't help you," Bob said. "All these fortifications, all these defenses—if the end comes, none of this will matter."

The whites of the Reverend's eyes grew brighter. He took a step back. "We are not trying to stop it. Who are you?" Under his breath, the priest began muttering some kind of incantations. Prayers.

They weren't going to help him, either.

"Embracing the end? Is that what you're doing?" Bob advanced on the old man. "This is a celebration of the destruction to come?"

Was the Commune involved in what was happening to him? Bob moved closer, tried to bridge the gap into the priest's mind, but the area was devoid of any technology he could hack into—every trace of the dark crystals wiped clean somehow—and there was no trace of smarticles or particles in the air. He had to rely on interpreting the old man's facial and body expressions.

Right now they expressed terrified fear, despite the glowering frown.

"Not destruction. The Apocalypse will be a revelation, the final disclosure of the hidden world. 'The lifting of the veil' was the meaning of 'Apocalypse' when John of Patmos wrote it down in Greek."

Another old man, sprawled in the dirt, came into Bob's mind. John of Patmos. "What do you know about Robert Baxter?" Bob asked. Did this priest know it was him inside his nephew's body? He watched the old man's face carefully.

Nothing. His face registered nothing but confusion.

Bob was about to ask, Then why didn't you let Robert Baxter into the Commune, if you don't know him? But that event hadn't happened yet in this world. Bob and Sid and Vince wouldn't arrive in their physical bodies for another week. They hadn't even left Atopia yet.

"And the Book of Pobeptoc?" Bob asked. It was the text that Mikhail Butorin had given Vince.

The look of confusion on the man's face deepened. He had no idea what Bob was talking about.

"The Gospel of Thomas?" Bob persisted. Another of the texts Butorin had brought up with Vince.

Now the old priest's face lit up. "Of course. The Gospel of Thomas: 'All those that understand my words shall not die,'" he quoted. "'When the inner becomes the outer, and the outer the inner. When hands become feet—'"

"I know the text," Bob interrupted.

"Then you know this was part of the Nag Hammadi libraries, primeval Gnostic texts dug up from the sands of Egypt in the 1940s, the same time the Dead Sea Scrolls were found. Hidden for thousands of years. Only one copy found, alongside the Gospels of Mary and—"

"Mikhail Butorin, do you know him?" Bob concentrated on the priest's face, watched for any sign of deception. Was this old man working with the Russian?

The man frowned, his eyes narrowing as he tried to understand what Bob might be getting at, what danger he might be in. He nodded.

Hair prickled on the nape of Bob's neck. Finally, something. "How?"

"He was one of the men that found and dug up the Nag Hammadi scrolls. A terrible cripple from what I recall. He must be dead by now . . ."

Bob's excitement deflated.

"But I do have something I think may interest you," the Reverend said.

Something happened in the old man's face. Some realization.

The priest pointed toward the back of the room. "Follow me." He walked past Bob and took a set of keys from his robe that he used to unlock a cabinet at the far end. He carefully lifted out a stack of yellowed papers. "The Voynich manuscripts. Do these mean anything to you?"

Bob inspected the papers. He'd heard of them; Vince had mentioned them. Bob leafed through a few pages. The edges of the paper crumbled. It was carbon-dated to the year 1404. Images of plants and animals, an indecipherable text nobody had been able to crack.

Except that Bob could read them instantly.

These were plants and animals from an alien world he had once inhabited, once upon a time long ago, in a world beyond distant. Just a whisper of a dream he could barely remember. He held up his hand, imagined webbed green skin between them, two suns in an emerald-blue sky.

"You are from Atopia, yes?" asked the Reverend.

Bob nodded, still engrossed in dredging up the memory of this other world. He flipped through the pages of the Voynich manuscripts.

"The ancient visions of a future and past where people live forever," the Reverend said. "Buddhist statues with many heads and hands, out-of-body experiences, does this not sound familiar? Unending cycles of existence? I will try to explain Apocalypse to you in terms you will understand."

Bob turned from the pages to look straight at the priest.

"If this life is a simulation," said the Reverend, "and I am using the term because you will understand it, then there is the possibility of eternal life. Yes? We will see our loved ones again when we die, go back into our young bodies. Are you not arisen yourself from the dead?"

The priest pulled away from Bob and began muttering prayers under his breath again. He then took a vial from a shelf, opened it, and dusted its contents into the air. "But what is the purpose of living life again? To what goal? Who is judging?"

"That's what I'm trying to find out. Why are you working with Butorin?"

"He was a searcher for the truth. As am I."

The air seemed to evacuate itself from the room. Bob's vision narrowed. What was the priest doing?

"Butorin's a monster," Bob said with a gasp.

"We are all monsters, each in our own way. The release of your Atopian technology will be the start of the unveiling, but yours is not the only one . . ."

The room faded to black.

Bob's mind collapsed.

12

A blanket of nighttime stars shimmered through the haze of the aerial plankton shield outside the Commune's perimeter.

"What did the old man do?" Sid blinked the fox's eyes.

"Pushed us out of Willy's body somehow," Bob replied.

One moment they'd been inside the Commune, inside of Willy's body, leafing through pages of the Voynich manuscripts, and the next instant Bob had had to latch their conscious point-of-view back into the fox. Their hold on the creature was slipping, the smarticle count in its bloodstream falling.

"So he exorcised us?" Sid retreated the fox to the edge of the forest.

The Reverend knew something he wasn't telling, but then Bob and Sid had snuck into the Commune under false pretenses. Still, the old man had some knowledge of the old machine, the dark crystals that Willy's body had gone on to investigate under New York after leaving. The same technology Terra Nova had been tracking, or had implanted—but one thing at a time.

"I didn't find anything unusual in Willy's body," Sid said. "I mean, not beyond the *usual* unusual. He had the copy of the POND data, but I unlocked it and found copies of lives you'd already lived. I did find out that it was you that told Wally to leave Atopia, though."

"I don't remember that." Bob's memories of his other lives were fleeting whispers. He didn't retain all the information, but rather impressions, dreams that dissipated like a wet smudge on a countertop on a hot summer day.

"That's what Wally said you'd say."

"Tyrel already admitted that he helped Wally leave Atopia." Breaching the security of Terra Nova was going to be even more difficult than the Commune.

"With Butorin's help," Sid said, "but apparently at your suggestion."

"We need to split up."

"Say it ain't so."

"Take us to Terra Nova," Bob said. "Straight along this timeline. Figure out how to get in."

"What are you going to do?"

"Talk to the Russian."

Cold clouds hung suspended over white-crested mountains. The Urals had borne the weight of glaciers of a hundred ice ages on their weary shoulders. In a saddle-shaped valley of scraped-smooth rock, a frost-blue lake reflected scudding clouds. A river snaked down from it, through an alluvial plateau dotted with scrub bush and scraggly pine eking out their existence before winter's furious return.

In the foothills below, the river met another, and in a clearing at their confluence was a small wooden cabin, freshly painted bright white in sharp relief to the muted landscape. Wisps of smoke curled from its chimney of rounded river stones set in cement. A barn stood guard beside the cabin, its wood beams gray and sagging under the weight of time. Bob materialized at the edge of the farm in a thicket of birch trees with bright yellow leaves announcing the fall season. He followed a muddy path toward the cabin. The hair on the back of Bob's neck prickled in the damp, fresh air, and his stomach grumbled at the smell of the fire smoke tinged with hints of something roasting inside.

Hunger was a perpetual feature of this private virtual world.

A man holding a huge ax stood next to the barn, his torso bare and muscular. He wore mud-spattered combat fatigues over black boots. A fringe of white hair ringed his bald head, beaded with sweat from the work of splitting wood. He shouldered the ax, sensing Bob's arrival in his private space. He insisted on people walking their way onto his farm. He liked boots in the mud.

Bob trudged through the muck and leaves up the main path. He'd had to make concessions to see Mikhail Butorin this quickly, had to let this timeline slide forward to just past his meeting with Vince again, and this time the meeting had been the same but slightly different. Each timeline he inhabited had its own peculiarities.

The man's face lit up, his glacial-blue eyes open wide amid the crinkled creases of his weathered face. "Come, come, my friend," he said in a thick Russian accent.

"We are not friends."

Mikhail Butorin shrugged in a Gallic motion borrowed from the way the French ignored something they didn't agree with. "But it is good to see you."

"I'm only here to get some answers."

"As am I."

"I find you disgusting."

The Russian laughed. "I have heard worse. Mostly from my wives."

Bob shouldn't have let his emotions slip. Somehow this man had something over Patricia. Trading insults wasn't going to help. "I meant your cult of Aesthetics."

"There is a reason to that madness, if this is your question. Cybernetic organisms with as little biological machinery as possible, to reduce interference from your nervenet technology." Mikhail seemed to ponder for a second. "To be honest, to reduce their frailty against a hostile world, in all its forms." Mikhail pointed his ax at the veranda of the small cabin, where he'd just had his discussion with Vince. He walked to the veranda, leading Bob forward, then took a shirt from the railing and pulled it on over his head. He indicated a chair across from a bare wooden table for Bob to sit at and sat across from him on a bench.

"So you're planning to fight the introduction of the Atopian pssi?" Bob asked.

"Only to protect myself. You know of Patricia's secret plans. Wouldn't you defend yourself?"

Truths and half-truths. The selfishness rang true: he *was* defending himself—if one included his interests in supplying weapons to all sides of the Weather Wars factions, and his flesh trade partners. He made it sound like an act of self-defense, when it was more of an act of war.

"Your cults predated any plans of Patricia's." Bob knew Butorin's organizations stretched back into the twentieth-century Russian mafia. "What did you have on her? Why did she let you into Atopia?"

"She needed my help."

"With Jimmy?"

Mikhail's face remained blank in a definite kind of way. "She didn't know about him until it was too late, but she suspected something was very wrong inside of Atopia. She *knew* something was coming. You saw her prediction models."

"Was it you? Were you trying to get control of Atopia?"

"As I said, she contacted me."

That didn't answer the question.

Bob tried to worm his way into Butorin's internal systems, but the man's security network was tight, if using the word "man" even made sense. One of the reasons he had asked to come here was to get as close as possible, to find at least one channel from here into his core systems, but he couldn't get a fix on where Butorin really was, and that made it difficult to focus any informational attacks.

"You and I are not so different," Mikhail said. He wiped the sweat from his brow with the back of one meaty hand. "I come here, to this representation of my childhood family's farm, to find myself. Lost in time. Like you, perhaps?" He smiled a knowing grin. "Here I reconnect with my physical body. To sweat. To feel pain."

"I am nothing like you."

"You do not trust me. Perhaps the time for some truth?" The old Russian shrugged again, almost in defeat. "So then I will start."

The hulking snow-capped peaks disappeared, and Bob's viewpoint spun upward into the sky. The blackness of space enveloped them, and they sped toward a dot of light. A satellite. Defended by a swarm of networked drones. The viewpoint pierced the main orbiting array, burrowed past layers of machinery to arrive at a circular vat. The folded membranes of gray matter. A brain floating in a viscous soup. Mikhail Butorin's brain.

"This is me, what is left of me," the old Russian said, his voice bereft of emotion. "I left the Earth behind many years ago, to spin endlessly in this dark vacuum. Years before that I lost the last vestiges of my physical body. So I think we might have something in common?"

The network of drones around the satellite spread out like an immune system, like Bob's splinters spreading out around him into the future and past, a network borrowed from Vince's own systems.

"Perhaps you could share some of your true self?" Butorin let Bob probe some of his outer networks, allowed him inside his mind just a little. "It was Patricia that unleashed the future-trap on your friend Vincent Indigo," he added.

"I know."

"She knew what she was doing, and it wasn't just to trap Vince. She was trying to share something with us."

"And what would that be?"

Again the Gallic shrug. "I am no politician. I am merely sharing what I can with you." Butorin opened up more of his mind, let Bob's probing fingers feel their way in.

"Why did you smuggle Willy's body out of Atopia?"

"You used it to get into the Commune, didn't you?"

"So you did it for me?"

"Patricia told you to come and find me, didn't she?"

"What did you want inside of Willy's body? You told Vince it contained something you'd been seeking for a long time."

The image of the brain in the vat faded, replaced with a statue of Buddha carved from a primordial meteorite. "Some called it Vril; the Nazis were obsessed with it. I was obsessed with it. Was tortured for my connection to it. The power over everlasting life and death. The Gospel of Saint Thomas: 'Whomsoever understands these words—'"

"'—will live forever,'" Bob said, completing the sentence for him.

The Russian's eyes twinkled. "You have been studying your scripture."

"That you dug up. The Nag Hammadi libraries."

"It found me, is how I would describe it." Mikhail smoothed down the fabric of his combat fatigues. "Do you believe in fate?"

"You mean destiny? Like there's no way to avoid what's coming?"

"I will phrase in another way. Do you believe the universe operates according to a definite set of rules, or is there ineffable randomness?"

It was a rhetorical question.

"If there is no randomness," Butorin continued, "then given initial conditions, a universe set in motion will tend toward a definite and unalterable conclusion. This is what I call fate."

"Determinism." It was a version of what Bob was already doing. He'd set the initial conditions of a universe, let it slide forward billions of years until one of them produced the same world he'd once known, the only one he was interested in.

Butorin nodded. "And no free will, because no matter what we think we are choosing, the path has already been set out. That freedom of choice we feel is just an illusion."

Was free will an illusion? No matter which way Bob turned, his adversary always seemed one step ahead. It always seemed that no matter what he did, the outcome was already determined. Was Mikhail revealing something to him? Bob retreated a few inches. "What are you saying?"

"On the other hand, if there is some inalienable randomness to the operation of the universe, then free will is no longer an illusion. But randomness in the mechanics of the universe is a sign that perhaps the universe we perceive is not real, is not the base reality."

"That's one interpretation." And one that was troubling Bob.

"Another is that free will is the mechanism that forms our universe, the same way that reality only crystallizes for a conscious observer."

"This is old ground you're covering."

"Is it?" The old Russian leaned back in his chair. "I believe we are all on our own paths, to glory, or to hell. Existence isn't just declarative, 'I think, therefore I am,' but exclamatory, 'Imagine! I am!'" He spread his arms wide and leaned forward, his voice lowered into a conspiratorial whisper: "And then the question of existence becomes interrogatory: What should I make of that? What does it mean to choose your meaning? What am I to make of my fellow humans? And, of course, of death . . . Why was I born if my life wasn't forever?"

"Existentialism," Bob whispered back, nodding despite himself. "Life has only the meaning that you give it."

"But this does not exclude the idea of God." The Russian knew Bob, or at least had assimilated enough background information to know how to push his buttons. "More than half of the world's passionate existential philosophers were also passionate religionists."

And also misguided, Bob thought but didn't say. "I didn't come here for a lesson in metaphysics."

The Russian smiled a languid grin and shrugged in that Gallic way again. "But I think perhaps you did. Do you really think that we are just passive laundry machines through which thoughts pass and are washed clean before the next cycle? That we have no free will?"

"Of course not."

"Then your reality is formed by your will."

Bob had had enough. "Why did you lie to Vince? Give him this Book of Pobeptoc?"

"That is the truth, the same truth as contained in the Book of Thomas."

"'Wal lie body is where the flesh eaters live?'" Bob quoted from the disputed text. "That led Vince to find Willy's body with the Papua New Guinea cannibal tribe. You're telling me this is from a two-thousand-year-old scroll you dug up in the desert?" Maybe this old Russian wanted them to find Wally, had done something to lead them down this path. Put something inside Wally. Was he the one pulling the strings?

"See for yourself." Butorin opened his mind, and Bob's networks assimilated his memories. "This is not the first time we have met, you and I," the Russian laughed. "It is so good to see you, my friend."

13

"Aren't we a strange little creature?" Sid said.

It wasn't a question.

Bob waved their antennule—a hermit crab's dense, toothbrush-like array of foreleg hairs—in the air to taste it. Though he could do little to change the physical characteristics of the crab's sensing system, he'd rewired the processing back end to watch for suspicious chemical markers. The master of metasenses deep in his work, inside a crab, a tiny hermit crab they'd positioned to hitch a ride on the snout of a right whale in a slow-motion attack on the Terra Novan defensive shield.

Nobody would suspect a crab.

This was a deep-cover infiltration that had been going on for months, with Bob's mind half-asleep inside a succession of hermit crabs that were born and died within this tiny microcosm of barnacles and seaweed attached to the whale's skin. He didn't trust his daemons to get him in close to Tyrel and Mohesha and Terra Nova. Not this close to the Destroyer, who was guiding the instance of Bob in this world across Africa right now.

"Ten thousand times larger, and we'd be a horror film star." Sid chuckled and flexed the hind four of their ten legs to get a better grip on the inside of the snail shell.

He stretched the crab's fore-stalks and tried to focus on the image of Terra Nova through the multiple lenses of the primitive eyes. The glass towers of Atopia's offshore rival shimmered on the horizon each time the whale breached the surface, while the hermit crab skittered around near its blowhole. Sid wanted to flit into the local wikiworld to get a better view, but it was too dangerous.

Bob's physical self in this world was coming to the Council meeting with Tyrel, about to plan the ill-fated attack on Atopia. He better not crowd himself. He couldn't let himself know another part of him was here, and he knew the Destroyer was very close. He was going to sacrifice this world once he contacted Tyrel—that much he knew was true, or was inevitable—but this was an incremental game, gleaning small bits of information before this world ended.

He just had to get in close enough.

The crab was too small for Bob to effect a proper data system, so he'd networked together a neural net of barnacles across the body of the whale. Controlling the "big guy" was a little more difficult—the whale's fifteen pounds of brain and hundreds of pounds of other connected gray matter were orders of magnitude larger than he usually dealt with. He couldn't control the whale directly but inserted a whale song into its auditory channels, one that led it on a meandering course toward Terra Nova. This hunk of blubber was chasing a baleen nymphet that really didn't exist. Welcome to the club.

"Did we really meet Mikhail before?" Sid asked as the whale dove down into the depths. He used their forelegs to get a better grip on a barnacle against the rushing water. "Was he telling the truth?"

"I have no memories of it," Bob replied. "In the next cycles, I'm going to dispatch daemons to watch him through time."

"But if he's our Destroyer, won't he see your daemons? Let them see whatever he wants us to see?"

"We need to widen our net slowly. Watch for inconsistencies."

"He wasn't lying about the Book of Pobeptoc," Sid said. "I infected the minds of a thousand other people and checked their memories. That thing existed."

"Or someone implanted the memories."

"Or that." Sid waved their antennules around in deliberation.

Pobeptoc—the literal translation of Robert in ancient Greek. The Book of Bob. Someone had implanted this deep in the history of this world. A critical nodal point in the game. Mikhail had answered all their questions in riddles, but he hadn't lied about this. He might have been the one to plant it, much deeper in history, if he was the Destroyer. What was his reason? Or did someone manufacture the memories?

Motive was emerging as the key factor in this mirror maze.

Why was the Destroyer doing what it was doing?

Was it the elimination of intelligence? The only time he'd spoken directly to the Destroyer was on his journey across the desert, but maybe this was all part of the illusion.

"Your using that time-cloaking encryption algorithm to hide the POND data makes sense now," Sid said. "Our moving back and forth through it, it ceases to have the same meaning."

Each time his daemons awoke him, the world was the same, but different. Each time he had to watch his other self go through the same motions, burying his mind under layers of drugs and apathy before waking up to confront the Destroyer. If he'd just been more aware the first time, perhaps he would have been able to stop this cycle of destruction. It disgusted him. He loathed his former self. It was easier this time—he just had to slide forward from his meeting with Mikhail Butorin, gliding over the surface of clear time.

The whale breached the surface again, the crystal towers of Terra Nova looming closer, but the angular black lines of the Atopian attack now appeared on the horizon as well. The final battle was about to begin again, the fight that precipitated the destruction of this world.

"Maybe we're overthinking this. Maybe it is Terra Nova," Sid said. "This is the beginning of the end for them. They lose, so maybe Tyrel ends this timeline. It was within their sphere of influence, this ending."

"Tyrel *is* the one trying to destroy Atopia," Bob voiced his thoughts in Sid's head. "The reality-skin infection that created the illusion of the storms, these dark crystals they knew about. Maybe it does all start with them."

"He seems all high and mighty, but powerful people can be awful in the things they do to retain power. To make sure nobody forgets them. Maybe he resented Patricia crossing the finish line first. If we're looking for a Destroyer, he is the one that tries to literally destroy Atopia. Like you said."

"So how do we get in?" Bob asked.

"Easy. Tyrel gives you the keys, remember? Let's sit back and watch the show, see if anything changes."

Bob watched himself leave the slums of Lagos, past the space power grid collectors and substations of the supercollider ring that first ended this Earth. He carefully inserted a tiny daemon inside the mind of the Bob coming aboard Terra Nova and again watched the Council meeting with the Terra Novan elders. The thought-plastic space opened up and molded itself around each attendee—Patricia's old student Mohesha, Tyrel, the other assembled elders, and Willy, his virtual presence wedged between avatars of Bob and Sid and Vince flanking them. Mikhail Butorin lurked in a dark patch of the shared sensory space where light seemed to come from within and without but didn't penetrate near him. This version of Mikhail had already met with another version of Bob, or perhaps he thought it was Bob himself. He must have known he was being watched and didn't reveal anything to Tyrel. The older gangster was used to the arts of deception.

"You have many questions." Tyrel brought the meeting to order. "As do we."

An image of an oceanic platform appeared in the shared meeting space. It was Atopian in design but looked nothing like Atopia itself. Its surface was angular, jet black. The attack platforms.

"The end is coming," said Tyrel.

Bob observed the meeting and compared it with copies of the previous versions in his memories.

Tyrel knew of the Great Destroyer, had said that this entity had destroyed a civilization on Earth two hundred million years before at the Great Permian Extinction, but Bob couldn't find any evidence of this. A lie? But why? The Terra Novan leader also knew about the dark crystals, about the advanced nervenet technology spreading around the planet in advance of the Atopian release. The technology of old crystals was not totally immune to detection; the Glasscutters of New York had been able to see it, as had Tyrel, as had Willy's proxxi—but perhaps because Tyrel and the old Reverend at the Commune had pushed him on that path. They both knew of the Destroyer, and the Reverend in the Commune had said Atopia's wasn't the only technology—and Tyrel had pushed Willy on his path to leave Atopia, had been instrumental in creating the unbreakable link into Willy's mind that forced him to leave.

The meeting was over, the final plans set in motion. Bob's other self had entombed itself in the oceanic transport, and Tyrel was giving him access to the core of the Terra Novan systems. Access that was keyed to Bob's cognitive systems. Sid used this to slip their full self from the network of barnacles coating the whale submerged just off Terra Nova. Bob's virtual self materialized in a flowering garden of begonias on a terrace of the main glass spire to watch the oceanic tanker disappear into the blue distance. He watched himself going to his own death.

"What are you doing here?" Tyrel appeared in the garden, his shock of white hair combed back, encircling his face to meet with the full beard, equally white. His face creased, his eyes open wide in fear or concern.

No alarms sounded.

"You gave me access to your internal networks," Bob replied.

He sensed Tyrel checking the metatags of his virtual presence, but this *was* Bob. Just a different version.

The old man's face furrowed deeper but remained unafraid. "But for the battle to come, not to return here. Your cognitive functions are supposed to be suppressed to approach Atopia. Why are you still awake?"

"I have more questions."

"Why did you not ask them in the meeting? You are putting the project at risk."

"Why did you keep the external channel for Willy's mind open? Were you trying to lure me here?"

"I already told you. To protect him."

At the meeting, Bob's other self had been almost demure. He hadn't had any reason to think Tyrel was lying to him. This time Sid and Bob unleashed an attack against Tyrel's systems, with full access to his networks. They scoured the Terra Novan databases for any inconsistencies. Bob knew the attack wouldn't go unnoticed and would trigger a confrontation with the Destroyer. He was pushing ahead the destruction of this world, but he needed only a few minutes.

"What was it in Willy's body that you wanted?"

"What are you doing?" Tyrel tried to exit the garden platform, but Bob had sealed the exits and trapped the man's presence inside a tight security blanket. In a short time, this would trip alarms.

"Was it the POND data?" Bob said.

The old man quit looking for ways to escape. "Why, what was in the POND?" he asked.

Again the answering of questions with questions. The warning Sid had decoded, just before this world had ended: "Don't let me kill myself." This was a message encoded deep within the POND. In a splinter of his mind, he watched the oceanic transport disappear over the horizon on its way to Atopia.

From his reaction, from what Bob could sense with his networks wrapped deep into Tyrel's, he didn't sense that the old man had been interested in the POND. Not really. But now Tyrel was.

Bob decided to try another tack. "Wally said he left because Jimmy was stealing minds, and you helped him escape. You said Jimmy was infected."

"As you said yourself."

"With what?"

"The Destroyer."

"And how did you know of this Destroyer?"

Tyrel hesitated. "The old texts. All of them. The study of eschatology. The end of days."

The words hit Bob's mind in a rush of cold black. "The Reverend at the Commune. You're working with him?"

"We work together." Tyrel hesitated again, but realized it was impossible to resist Bob.

"To destroy Atopia?" Bob felt his fury rising. The Communes had been designed as fortresses, as had this place. Antitechnological, and both opposed to Atopia.

"If Jimmy was infected by this Destroyer, why not just eliminate Jimmy?" Bob asked.

"Because he was not the source of the infection."

"Because you were," Bob stated, but there was no reaction from Tyrel. "You and Mohesha were the source of these dark crystals."

"We were not. They must be destroyed."

More fury erupted inside of Bob. "But they hold the memory of all human lives, everyone who has ever existed here."

The look on Tyrel's face shifted from shock to puzzlement. "How do you know that?" His internal networks were still struggling against

Bob's incursion. "There is no register of you coming in through the networks from the oceanic tanker. How are you here? How do you see inside the crystals?"

"I'm asking the questions, Tyrel. How did *you* see into them?" Bob still suspected it was through Terra Novan technology.

The old man shrugged. "We could only read data tracks going into them, like a black box whose external connections we could monitor. The internal systems are vastly superior to anything we can understand. It is like a caveman seeing an airplane for the first time."

"At the meeting you said the Destroyer killed off an ancient civilization on Earth. How do you know this?"

Again the Terra Novan leader hesitated. "The Voynich manuscripts. We managed to decode some of them. The images of green animals and plants, humanoid figures. The star charts inside dated them to an early period, hundreds of millions of years ago."

Bob took a second to process. That wasn't *this* world, wasn't Earth—it was another planet, thousands of light-years distant. "How did you know nervenet technology was convergent evolution?" The only way he could have known this was by skipping from one universe to another, by following the same path Bob had followed.

"Because we simulated our own societies inside our machines."

"What?"

Tyrel's networks nudged his and opened a communication channel. A view of a simulated Earth spun into Bob's mind. A world simulation currently in the early twenty-first century, seven billion human minds in near-perfect simulation. Some less than others, some more detailed than others. Some merely zombies presenting a mindlike form.

"We have run hundreds of simulations, and each time, nervenet technology tends to evolve as the humanoid minds move from biological to informational substrates. At that point we need to terminate the simulation."

"So you destroy billions of souls?"

"Sad, yes, but no pain. They just wink out of existence. And it is too dangerous."

"Dangerous?"

"A problem of finite computational resources. The laws of physics that we simulate have to have a finite set of points within a finite volume, a noncontinuous space-time. The entities begin to notice unusual distributions of energy in discrete points. A granularity we cannot hide, these flaws in the simulation. Eventually, some of the entities try to escape, to jump out of their world and into ours."

A breeze blew through the garden, spreading a rain of red petals from the towering begonias.

Tyrel smiled. "The answer to Fermi's paradox, young man. The question that has been haunting you. Why is it that nobody else is 'out there'? Perhaps because there *is* no out there. In our simulations, we even created alien races for them to talk to. Perhaps our creators didn't bother to take the same steps."

A noose seemed to tighten around Bob's neck, strangling off the oxygen that he didn't even breathe anymore—or perhaps the tenuous ledge his mind found its perch on narrowed, the maddening chasm below beckoning. What if his Destroyer was just some entity operating on a higher level of simulation? Simply switching the world off when Bob escaped or got too close to the truth. How could he fight that?

Bob waited before asking, "You have evidence of this?"

Tyrel's smile trembled. "The evidence is everywhere, and nowhere."

"Stop with the riddles. Just answer my questions."

"There are two interpretations of what we perceive as our physical world. If any of the thirty-plus constants in the physical laws weren't exactly as they are now, life could not exist. So, first, we can take the anthropic argument and say that we only exist because conditions are exactly the way they are. This implies trillions and trillions of other random attempts at universes, devoid of life, where no consciousness exists. Which makes it difficult or impossible for wave functions to collapse."

"That's possible."

"Possible, but without any purpose. And if there is no purpose for consciousness, then why does reality remain fuzzy until a conscious observer intervenes?"

"Purpose implies some kind of creator."

"Exactly my point. Someone or some*thing* that created conditions to be just right."

"But then where does it start? It must start at some point."

Tyrel stood still, didn't try to fight Bob's attacks against his internal networks anymore.

"I need some answers!" Bob tore into the Terra Novan archives, searching for anything that might show Tyrel was lying. "You put us onto this path, pushed me to confront Jimmy. What is your connection to Mikhail Butorin? You both infiltrated Atopia and tried to destroy it."

The Terra Novan leader's shoulders slumped.

"What are you hiding?" Bob demanded. The hesitations before answering all his questions. It was obvious there was something he wasn't telling him.

Tyrel retreated a few steps, sat down on a weathered wooden bench, and inspected the ground. "Patricia was the one that invited us inside the firewalls of Atopia. We didn't infiltrate, as you say."

"Then she knew of your trap. She knew about the reality-skin infection to destroy Atopia?"

The old man shook his head. "It was too late by then. But it was Patricia that first discovered the dark crystals, this alien technology. She embedded part of it inside the Atopian technology. It was what gave her the power. I tried to tell her to stop, but in her arrogance . . ."

"But why?"

"Her simulations, her future prediction models. Everything came up in destruction. As you know. As we do. She studied the theology and philosophy of the final events of the history of the world. She recognized that when humanity breached the posthuman wall, it always ended, one way or the other. She was obsessed with trying to stop it, wanted to place the control in her own hands."

"So you were trying to stop her?"

"She created sanctuaries where we were protected, to study the old texts."

"You mean the Communes?"

"The Killiams, and Willy's family, the McIntyres, are old family trees that began in Scotland, hundreds of years ago. Did you not see the connection . . . ?"

"What are you saying?"

Tyrel raised his eyes from the ground to look straight at Bob. "Killiam was our high priestess of eschatology, our pastor of the end of the world. Or the unveiling. Depending on what you believe." He exhaled long and hard. "But now it is too late, she is gone."

Bob gritted his teeth. "Nobody is ever really gone. Not in my world."

14

"A great evil will consume you all!" a deranged man yelled from between tangled teeth.

His mottled red face barely restrained a threatened apoplectic fit as he perched atop an upturned four-gallon paint can in the Speakers' Corner near Marble Arch and Hyde Park. It was early morning, halfway around the world from Atopia, and the usual collection of crackpots and doomsayers had already installed themselves for the afternoon tourist crowds. The steady drone of the automated passenger traffic hummed over the electric crackle of London's city center. Pigeons fought over scattershot birdseed thrown by the man's hunchbacked wife.

The old man atop the paint can wheezed asthmatically and rolled his eyes up to the damp skies before returning to Earth to hunt through the crowd. His watery gaze fixed on to the virtual avatar of Vince Indigo, who stopped walking to stare back at the man.

"A great evil is already consuming you, sir," the old man whispered.

And then he pointed at Bob, ghosting right behind Vince, and screeched to the crowd, "A *great evil* is upon us!"

The old man's already distended pupils widened as he peered at Bob, even though he should have been invisible. A small part of his mind was here, transported back along the timeline into a new world, awakened by his flock of daemons. He hid in surveillance mode, but sometimes people seemed able to see him: crazy people, the infirm, the spiritual. When he passed, they looked up and noticed, either his presence or others things he saw, too, glitches in the machine, echoes of people in the wrong time and place. Just like him.

Vince thought the old man was pointing at him, when in fact he was pointing at Bob, hidden in the pigeon fluttering past. Vince hunched his shoulders inward and shuffled through the crowd, while Bob pushed his carrier bird higher to watch from a distance.

The crazy man's eyes followed the pigeon into the sky.

Today was the day Patricia Killiam would lie to her old friend Vince, and Bob wanted to watch it firsthand.

Ahead in this timeline, Vince's future selves kept watch to thread the needle of safety that was keeping him alive against the barrage of potential deaths unleashed by Patricia's networks. A microcosm of Bob's own situation, the similarities were hard to ignore—replacing Vince's death with the deaths of entire universes that Bob tried to navigate, but then the death of a person was the death of his or her entire universe. Was Bob's attacker the same as Vince's? Was Patricia even aware of what she might have unleashed?

From high overhead, Bob watched Vince wind his way through the green-and-white-striped loungers at this edge of Hyde Park and follow the path that tracked the Serpentine.

At the end of the path waited his old friend.

"So what's all this on Phuture News about you dying today?" Patricia Killiam said to Vince as his avatar met hers near the old site of the Crystal Palace, physically gone for two hundred years but its virtual presence gleaming in the wet sunlight of their shared meeting space.

"The news of my death has been greatly exaggerated," Vince joked back.

Bob circled and watched the exchange.

Rewinding time to come back and observe Patricia Killiam had been painful, but "rewinding" wasn't the right word. To his conscious stream, it had that effect, but to another part of him, a part that he submerged when he awakened, the journey was one through the birth of an entire universe, of billions of years of time. Each time it became more difficult, more painful, the submergence longer.

And each time he lost something of himself.

Patricia Killiam accepted Bob's ping on its first bounce. Outside the hull of Atopia, the imaginary hurricanes converged, what Bob considered the end of the first cycle of events. Jimmy Scadden was about to light up the slingshot batteries to burn a hole through the imaginary storms. Everything imaginary, except America's nuclear arsenal, pointed directly at them.

That was as real as anything.

The muted atmosphere of Patricia's waiting room suffused into Bob's senses, the paneled walls and bottle-green lampshades and paintings of ships in storms. It stank of oiled wood, old carpets, and cigarettes—one of which Patricia lit up. Its smoke wreathed around her head. It felt like an accountant's office, perhaps, one where the taxes were far past due. Her hair done up in a tight gray bun, she was dressed in her usual business suit, but not inhabiting the much younger version of herself she usually did. She sat there, shriveled, in a real-to-life virtual presentation of her hundred-year-old body.

"I know everything," Bob said, but not angry, not blurting out as he had done before at this moment.

He'd hijacked the mind of Bob in this world, right at the moment when Atopia was about to pierce the reality-skin infection from Terra Nova. His physical body was still in neural fusion with Nancy, their bodies wrapped around each other in a tub of ice water, surrounded by Sid and Vince, down in the lower infrastructure of the seastead, below Purgatory in the entertainment district, near the routing core of Atopia. Their together-mind was still spread wide, expanded throughout the entire Atopian ecosystem.

Patricia's face remained blank. "Everything?" She tipped her cigarette into an ornate crystal ashtray.

The feeling of déjà vu was almost overpowering. How many times had he confronted her? How many different outcomes had he tried to use to push the future timeline one way or the other to reveal the Destroyer? This time he'd built a defensive network into the future and past, borrowed from Vince's own designs. Spies and agents searching for dangerous technology that could end this universe. One was the Extreme Light Infrastructure project that generated pulses of light a trillionth of a second long, at intensities so highly ionized the vacuum created positrons and electrons from nothing. It was the same process as began universes—and destroyed them. People didn't understand what they were playing with. Or maybe some of them did. Maybe one in particular. He had to find out who.

"How was your meeting with Tyrel?" Bob asked.

He'd inserted himself just as she'd finished her desperate meeting with Tyrel and Mohesha, imploring them to stop the hurricanes from smashing Atopia. He'd watched the meeting again as a fly on the wall—literally. Patricia still thought the hurricanes outside were real. Terra Nova and Tyrel knew she'd been plotting with Mikhail Butorin, but they'd been planning this with him as well. Thick as thieves. No wonder this first cycle ended so badly.

Patricia's face still didn't give anything away. "We're about to ignite the slingshots, Bob. I'm a little busy right—"

"You're less busy than you think. You're about to die."

"I think we're all about to die."

"I mean you in particular."

"Is that a threat?"

Bob observed her every nuance and waited. Getting back to this point had been excruciating, the memory of the suffocation in time a weight that pressed against his mind. He needed to remember everything. He needed to get as much information as possible.

"I already know I'm going to die," Patricia said in the silence. "My doctors—"

"It's not a failure of your medical systems. It's your star pupil, Jimmy. He's the one that's killing you. He killed his family, wormed his way into mine. He's taking control of Atopia. Right now."

Her eyes remained steady, but she tipped the cigarette and her hand trembled. A surprise but also not a surprise, he saw in her eyes.

"Why did you accept my ping so quickly?" The initial time he'd passed through the first cycle, she'd responded to his message request without hesitation, yet she'd been in the middle of meeting Tyrel at the same time as trying to stop the destruction of Atopia. Why would she give Bob a moment of her time so freely?

She didn't hesitate. "My proxxi, Marie, detected you and Nancy in the process of fusing your minds near the routing core." A sad smile fluttered across her face before it returned to confrontational blankness. "You spread your minds through the Atopian data centers, you used this opportunity—"

"To find answers."

"It was very smart."

"We know your secret."

"Just one?" Patricia exhaled a halfhearted laugh and leaned forward to stub out her cigarette with focused determination. "Hardly a secret when hidden in plain sight. More of an emperor's new clothes, where everyone is the king—"

"By giving everyone everything they ever wanted," Bob interrupted. This part of the story was a well-worn rut. "Turn them into addicts. Hook the world on your virtual crack."

"Addiction . . ." Patricia said the word slowly, turned it around in her mouth. "The word comes from the Latin word *addictus* for someone you owe money to—and because you owe them, you become a slave." She leaned back in her chair and assumed a thoughtful professorial pose. "Addiction implies slavery, and of course we think of drugs when we say this. But it also applies to anything that we use to fill that void inside. So my real aim, the question I am trying to pose to the world: What is the void inside of you?"

All Bob felt inside was a void.

What was it made of? Nothing. Literally nothing.

"And despite the intrigue," Patricia continued, "there is a very good reason—"

"You mean to stop Armageddon." Bob suppressed the image of the office and spun their viewpoint into space, to show a thousand Earths burning under future wars. Patricia's own future projections. "But you have miscalculated. You have tipped the world into the Apocalypse."

"I'm saving billions of lives."

"By sacrificing millions of billions of others, even more, that you can't even imagine. You have no idea what you have unleashed."

Patricia's eyes narrowed. "I'm trying to stop destruction," she protested, and then after processing his words: "What do you mean?" She wrested control of their visual environment back, the scenes of disaster replaced with the wood paneling of her office.

"The Apocalypse is not destruction, but the unveiling," Bob replied. "Don't play games anymore, Professor Killiam. Tyrel told me. You are the high priestess of eschatology. You have been studying the events of the end of the world for longer than you worked on synthetic reality or artificial intelligence."

She looked at him incredulously, but a crack appeared in her blank-faced impassivity. "When did you speak to him?"

Bob paused before answering, "Not yet in this timeline. Not yet in this world. But I have talked to him, at great length, about everything to do with you, Patricia. No more games."

They stared at each other, each trying to assess what exactly was happening. She lit another virtual cigarette and fidgeted with it. "Are you really Robert Baxter?"

He'd felt her checking and rechecking his metatags since the moment he'd materialized in her office, under her security blanket. He pulled his own high-density security blanket around him in this world.

"I am Robert Baxter, yes."

"My student?"

"I am a version of him."

"I see." She tipped her cigarette again, and he noticed her hand wasn't shaking anymore. "Whatever you intend, we don't have much time."

Now was the moment to push, to change this timeline. "These storms aren't real," Bob explained. "They were implanted by Terra Nova. By your student Mohesha. The warning in the POND data, that's a warning from me. To stop you."

"The POND data?" Now her stone-faced facade broke completely. "How is that even . . . how do you know all this?"

Through his metasenses, Bob felt the slingshot weapons powering up. In other runs through the end of this first cycle, he had fed Jimmy information that the hurricanes weren't real. The moment the slingshots were activated, America destroyed Atopia. He needed to keep it here for a few seconds longer. He didn't feed the information to Jimmy yet.

"You lied to me before," Bob said. "You said you didn't have anything to do with Willy."

"When did I say that?"

"The last time we had this conversation."

"Never had this—"

"You didn't tell me you knew Reverend McIntyre. That you were a founder of the Communes. That's why you sent Willy there."

Her perplexed look shifted into a kind of fear, but for a woman already comfortable with her death, the worry on her face was that she'd been desperately wrong about something.

"You knew about Communes," Bob continued, "about their cult of the Apocalypse. And I know you let Mikhail Butorin infiltrate Atopia. How do you know of the Destroyer?"

"The . . . ah . . . Destroyer?" At first she looked like she didn't understand, but her face dawned with a light of recognition. "That was the idea of Ignacius McIntyre, the Reverend, you call him. One we entertained when I was very young. That was a lifetime ago."

"You helped create Communes."

"'Create' is a strong word. I helped them with the technology that protects them." She wiped her face with one hand. "Did you and Jimmy—"

"Kill you for this? No, he's acting alone. Or, not alone . . . That's what I'm trying to find out."

"In the meeting I just had with Tyrel," Patricia said slowly, "he said I've unleashed an unspeakable evil. You just used those words again."

"Tyrel told you to stop," Bob replied. "You are the one engineering this whole thing. Now I can't escape."

In the world outside, the imaginary hurricanes tore against the virtual hull of Atopia, but the system core powering the slingshots in the real world had almost reached its peak output. American defense systems had almost reached their tripping point. Atopia was just dozens of miles from their shore and not responding to any distress or emergency calls.

Bob took hold of Patricia's sensory networks. "Let me show you . . ."

He pushed their viewpoint back out of the office, and then splintered into a dozen, then hundreds, and then thousands of universes he'd lived in: past worlds, future worlds, alien worlds. A shared vision floated between them, of lumbering green creatures, mouths full of fern, a sky with two suns, and hands with webbed green fingers.

Had he revealed too much? If Patricia was the Destroyer, then he was revealing some of his innermost secrets, so he still held back. Offered just enough to demonstrate his point. He didn't think this version of Patricia was his enemy, but then he'd been wrong about her before, and traces of her existed everywhere he traveled, even in the nervenets of alien worlds. One thing he was sure of, this release of information was enough to trigger the end of this world—so he had to destroy the evidence.

Patricia's mind absorbed the data streams.

The Atopian weapons systems flashed online. The slingshot batteries opened fire and tore a wall of plasma into the atmosphere around them.

"You're saying . . . so you have come . . . *back* in time?" Patricia said the words haltingly.

Even though he'd told her that the hurricanes were reality-skin infections, she still didn't understand the implications of the slingshots firing. She was still focused on Bob.

"Not back. Sideways. Into other universes. Something is chasing me, something unleashed from Atopia into the multiverse."

"This Destroyer?"

Bob nodded.

"And what do you want from me?"

"Am I in a simulation?"

"*In* a simulation?"

"One of the time loop sims that you've trapped Vince inside of. I know about that, too. Is what's happening to me just an endless series of your doomsday simulations? Or is this real?"

Time was something Bob had had altogether too much of, and yet here, in the ultimate moment, he had too little. Already America's defensive networks had greenlighted a tactical nuclear strike against Atopia. Bob hadn't fed Jimmy the information about the hurricanes being simulations. The slingshots blazed. In one small corner of his mind, he watched Vince shepherding Nancy and his mother and father onto the passenger cannon. They'd escape, but not the million other souls aboard.

"I wish this were a simulation," Patricia said after a pause.

She still had no idea what was happening outside. The security blanket was pulled tight around this private meeting space, shielding them from a barrage of emergency calls from the outside.

"Because the only logical alternative," Patricia continued, "is that humankind doesn't survive the transition to posthuman society—which we now stand on the brink of. Why? This is the question I have been trying to answer."

From Vandenberg Air Force Base, six tactical nuclear missiles rattled out of their silos. Bob could still stop them, could initiate their self-destruct sequences, but he needed more information. Was this world real or not? Was she in control? "You need to stop what you are doing."

"I can't stop it," Patricia replied.

An admission of truth? A splinter of Bob's mind watched the missiles arc into the clear blue Californian sky.

"At the end of the twentieth century," the Atopian founder continued, "the entire computing power of our planet was about the same as a single human mind. And now, a hundred years later, we have one hundred trillion times that capacity. Simulating a human brain in a computer requires about a million billion operations per second. Two billion seconds in eighty years means the experience of an entire human life can be reduced to a million billion billion simple calculations. Only one hundred billion humans have ever lived on this Earth, so all of humanity can be reduced to a simple sequence of operations, compressed into a split second of execution time."

Why was she wasting time in a history lesson? "Ancestor simulators. That's what you're talking about. Tyrel said he was running them."

"Together with me. Our networks have simulated hundreds of thousands of human civilizations, and capacity is expanding exponentially—but this is only the beginning. The theoretical limits of computation allow that a that single kilogram of atoms could process a hundred quindecillion operations per second—that's ten to the fiftieth power—meaning just a bucket of water could be used to simulate a *million billion* entire human histories, *every single second*."

The missiles pierced into the purple-black of space over the coast of America.

"We don't have much time," Bob said. "What can't you stop?"

"This process. Humankind has been doubling its information processing capacity every few years for hundreds of years now. It's a convergent evolutionary process that spontaneously occurs in intelligent species—"

"And intelligence is the root of suffering?" Bob borrowed the phrase from his memories of the priest, or perhaps priestess. He was close now.

Patricia nodded. "I suppose it is."

"Tyrel said that organisms inside the worlds you create always figure out they are in a simulation. That some of them try to escape. That you terminate the worlds when they do. Is this what you're doing? Why are you doing this to me?"

The missiles reached the zenith of their ballistic path and began to descend. The nose cones split open, spilling dozens of tiny warheads into space. They began their arcing journey down to the distant dot of Atopia. Bob had the destruct sequences keyed into his networks. His fingers hovered over them.

"I'm not doing anything to you," Patricia said, her voice soothing.

"But everything always leads back to *you*!"

Patricia leaned forward in her chair, tried to reach for Bob's hand. "Our program . . . we had no choice. Why does humanity not make it past the postbiological inflection point?"

"That's just a theory."

"I needed to push the edges of reality." Patricia closed her eyes. "We've seen echoes of you, Bob, everywhere in our networks. I thought it was a glitch—some kind of error—but I see now." She opened her eyes.

Bob stared straight at her. "When Atopian nervenet technology is released, something mutates in the evolutionary explosion and escapes into the multiverse. I think it's you, Patricia. I think you are terminating worlds, trying to end the suffering of intelligence. Trying to stop creatures from understanding they're not real."

"That's not what this is."

"I need to get back into my physical body. I can't take this anymore. I need to know. Is *this* a simulation?" He banged her desk with one hand, realizing the irony of being in a simulated world but demanding to know if it was real or not, but she knew what he meant: Was the world he knew with her real?

"There is no subjective difference for a simulated mind," Patricia replied quietly.

The splinter of Bob's mind following the warheads watched them sink into the atmosphere, the viewpoint of the sky gaining color. The passenger cannon pod with Nancy and Vince and his family aboard had cleared the area, but only seconds remained for him to abort the warheads.

He stood and towered over the shriveled figure of Patricia Killiam. "Why are you wasting time? Why not answer me?" he yelled. He'd tried to remain calm. Done his best. Failed.

"Are we in a simulation?" Patricia repeated his question, her voice low. She answered herself. "No, this is not a simulation. There are ways I've been able to verify our base reality—"

"How?"

"But . . ."

The warheads glittered in the skies over Atopia.

"But what?" Bob demanded.

"As part of the experiment of Atopia, we developed physical bodies for virtual beings." The words tumbled out of Patricia's mouth in an uncharacteristic rush. "Maintaining a living, breathing body is environmentally expensive, so we decided to share them." She paused. "Like ride-sharing automobiles."

"Why are you telling me this?"

"Because I created you," Patricia whispered.

"You . . . what?" A floodgate opened in the back of Bob's mind, a black terror rushing in again.

"This world is real, but you never were."

The last threshold was breached, but Bob didn't respond, didn't deactivate the incoming weapons. The warheads triggered their detonation sequences overhead. A splitting white light enveloped Atopia.

Patricia's gaze was steady in the last instants before she was incinerated, her voice firm: "You are our child, Bob, but you were never human."

Part 2

15

The Engineer circled her viewpoint around the circumference of the Project. The dark mass of millions of planet-size photonic arrays worked perfectly. They pulled out almost every photon emitted from the hot blue sun at their center to channel its energy along the hubs. Dense streams of microwave radiation flowed outward to one of the collectors, a funnel that focused the power densities—but carefully, she didn't want to ionize the vacuum. A shimmering tunnel of negative energy opened and punched a hole through time and space.

A tiny probe, invisible to the naked eye, waited at the mouth of the newly created wormhole.

She checked the qubit probes. The wave front of destruction approached, but she still had a few hours. Over four hundred years of working toward this single goal, and she'd made it with hours to spare—but hours were an eternity.

If it worked.

"Hello."

Someone materialized in one of her visual channels. An Umebak female, with drooping ventral lobes, but clear ovoid eyes that were unmistakable. The Engineer stared back into her *own* eyes, but a version of herself she wouldn't see for nearly a hundred years.

"It seems it worked?" she asked herself.

"It seems it did," her other self replied, a few seconds later.

The wormhole had opened a direct connection of light-seconds to Sood, the primeval homeworld, which was forty-two light-years away in flat space-time. Splintered parts of the Engineer's mind were distributed through all the Umebak worlds within the hundred-light-year informational sphere their race had spread into, but communication between her disparate parts was limited to the speed of causality. The part of her that just appeared in her mindspace usually had a question-response lag of eighty-four years. Shortened now to two seconds.

Her mind began reassimilating itself.

Images of lovers her other self had taken in the last eighty years, as their physical body had morphed from one chrysalis to the next. It was a process only carried out on Sood, to migrate from one physical body to the next. In the periphery, such nonsense was frowned upon as wasteful. The flood of familiar feelings and sensations tingled the Engineer's senses.

Was it real to her?

The question of the nature of reality was always of central importance to the Engineer.

Ever since she developed the first nervenet, the question of whether reality was "real" or a simulation went from metaphysical to practical. When the technology to run sensory-realistic simulations of the past first appeared, at first they were called games.

But the *presence* knew the games were dangerous. Simulating intelligent creatures inside these gameworlds led down paths that couldn't be closed, so she shut them down. Outlawed the running of ancestor simulators, of gameworlds that matched too closely the Umebak, of any self-running simulations with entities that were self-aware.

Banned them as a dark art.

But of course there were those that persisted.

If there was no difference in subjective experience for a biological organism—simulated or not—then the requisite detail of simulation was at the level of synapses. A computational device could run simulations of neural machinery that gave rise to consciousness, and therefore reality. It was just a quick step on the evolutionary ladder for computational organisms to gain awareness of self, and then awareness of their place in the cosmos—and this unleashed the desire to know their creator.

The endless circle of life.

The Council wanted an answer to the question of why nobody else was out there, but the Engineer knew there were but two answers: either they were in a simulation, and thus nobody else was out there because there was no out there—or no civilizations had survived the transition to postbiological, but in that case, what stopped them?

The Umebak had survived in the limbo just beyond the postbiological stage for five hundred years, but only because of the *presence* that the Engineer felt inside her. That *presence* forbade the ancestor simulators, forbade the games. The Council wanted to know what danger it faced, but the question the Engineer wanted to answer: Where did it all end?

"Engineer, it is good to see you." The Primary Vollix appeared in her sensory frames. This wasn't the near-space Vollix, but the central version of the homeworld. "Congratulations are in order."

"Thank you."

Though the wormhole was only a thousandth of an inch wide, the Engineer sensed physical objects amassed in the empty space around Sood.

"We will now be taking control," said the Vollix, "per the Council agreements."

"I haven't finished my tests yet," protested the Engineer.

She worked furiously in the background even as her networks bartered with the Council representative.

"What are the probes for?" the Vollix asked. "Those weren't part of the design specifications."

"There is a lot I haven't been able to communicate, Primary Vollix."

She had to buy time. She'd already opened distortions to other Sood worlds and expected to feel a warm rush of sensory information as she connected with the other parts of herself at each distant shore, but one by one, each of the distortions yielded nothing. Just empty space.

Then, not empty.

"Engineer!" her doppelgänger screamed in wide-spectrum distress.

She delivered a new spread of data. The very last probes, just light-minutes distant, had registered anomalous results. Her doppelgänger had decided to check all the qubits as the culmination of the project approached. A random hunch. Another wave front had appeared. Centered on a moon of the first gas giant orbiting just behind the sphere of the Project. Something had invaded her space, something she had missed.

How was it possible? The Engineer's mind raced, reconstructed the new data. She didn't have hours.

Only minutes remained.

Perhaps seconds.

16

A weak sun struggled over the horizon, illuminating twin sentinels towering thousands of feet over an empty harbor, witnesses to an oil slick spreading its rainbow stain around the Statue of Liberty. Down the East River, in the quiet air, pillars of smoke rose in smudges from flames gorging on derelict apartment buildings. A trio of ragged children played on a rubble pile between the burned-out shells of cars. The signal weakened, and the daemon reversed course to sweep back up the ghost-empty concrete canyons of Manhattan.

In the lower half of the island, it found its mark and zoomed down to street level. Inert bodies lay strewn across the cement between piles of garbage and empty bottles. A yellow-stained newspaper stuck to the sidewalk proclaimed, "Ford to City: Drop Dead!" One of the crumpled bodies attracted the daemon, the scent of death and decay overpowered by something more primal. Something more ancient. The man's face was pressed against the cold cement, ragged stubble on his chin. A spot of drool spilled from his open mouth—he was still alive, but barely. The sour tang of alcohol only just overpowered the stink of urine and feces.

The daemon checked its internal systems: Was this some postapocalyptic wasteland?

No.

It was New York, 1973.

A preapocalyptic wasteland.

"Buddy. Hey, buddy." A stubble-faced police officer kicked the man again, but gently this time. "Time to get up."

The fat man groaned and wiped spittle across his face with the back of a hand. One glazed eye opened for an instant to take in New York's Finest. It closed tight again. "Screw off." He rolled onto his other side and curled in a fetal ball.

The officer tipped back his cap, clucked, shook his head, and looked up and down the Bowery. Nothing else moved. Not even a rat in the garbage piled at the corner of Canal. Vaporous mist rose from a manhole cover in the middle of the street. He leaned down to grab the man under his shoulders, dragged him against the metal grating of an abandoned storefront, and tried to prop him upright. He had to hold his breath to stop from gagging at the stench. He put his own back against the wall and slid down to sit with the bum.

"You can't keep doing this," the officer said as he pulled out a pack of cigarettes. He offered one, but with no response shrugged and lit it himself. "This isn't helping anyone."

The bum groaned and pushed himself up a little, tried to straighten the greasy lapels of his sport coat.

"You know how long it took me to find you?" The officer took a puff and let the smoke curl out of his mouth. "You can't just—"

"None of this is real." The bum half opened his watery, bloodshot eyes to fix them on the policeman. "And give me one of those."

The officer gave the vagrant his own lit cigarette and took out the pack to light another.

"I'm not even real," coughed the bum. He took a drag and then hacked up a ball of sickly-green phlegm. He spat it out onto the sidewalk. "You're not even Sid. Not the real one."

"Come on, Bob, there's no need to be mean-spirited. I think, therefore I am, right? I'm thinking, so here I am; it's as simple as that. And you brought me on this trip with you. I'm as much of Sid as you'll let me be." Policeman-Sid blew his cheeks out in a long sigh. "I'm having a tough time, too, but I'm trying to help."

Bob-bum giggled, but it came out as more of a wet burp and hacking cough. "You want to help? Go get a copy of Vicious, and let's hit the town. East Village is just up the street. This is the New York of Lou Reed and Patti Smith, man. Screw this. Let's get messed up."

Sid-cop inspected the burning tip of his cigarette. "You know how long it took to find you?" he repeated.

"I know. Hundreds of years," Bob said. "And I've been right here the whole time."

The buildings around them began to morph and shift in time. Bob took control of their viewpoint and whisked Sid back through all the human drunks he'd cohabitated with on this spot, within this single-block stretch of concrete. Back a hundred years and the scene shifted into a dirt road, the buildings of concrete and brick disappearing into ramshackle wooden structures, and then further back in time, the area was overcome by trees of a dense forest.

"Did you know that Bowery is the oldest street in Manhattan?" Bob said. "When the Dutch first got here, they called the natives they met the Manhattos, but it was the Lenape tribe."

The drunk and the cop now leaned with their backs to a gnarled oak. They watched a young Lenape rolling around in the leaves. He giggled and pulled a pile of twigs toward him.

"Booze was hard to find back then, but mushrooms . . . there are always mushrooms in a forest." Bob kept his eyes on the writhing young man. "Before the Europeans arrived, the Bowery was a Lenape trail through the forest that traversed from the tip of Manhattan all the way along it. The Dutch used the trail, called it 'bouwerij' road, which is their name for farm. When this was the New Netherlands . . ."

Sid took back control of their visual channels and forced the scene into the present. The bleak concrete returned. "This is a nice history lesson, but—"

"The new nether regions of the world," Bob continued. "Imagine that—"

"You're drunk."

"As you should be. It was the thing we were really best at, when we were friends."

"We still are friends."

"Let me ask you a question. Does any of this *really* feel real to you?" Bob-bum held his cigarette out, then burned it into the lily-white skin of his forearm.

"That's not very nice to do to the owner of that body," Sid-cop said, his protective instincts stirring. "You're really hung up on this 'real' thing, aren't you?"

"Because everything is pointless otherwise."

"The only meaning to life is the one that you give it," Sid pointed out. "Isn't that what you always told me?"

"My life has no meaning."

"Because you're not giving it one. You *had* one. You dragged me out here for it."

"I don't even really have a life!" Bob-bum's vein-riddled face turned beet red, the tendons in his neck straining out. "You trying to make this *my* fault? Go away. Leave me alone. I only said that stuff when I was happy."

"You were taking drugs then, too, as far as I can remember."

"Happy-*er*, then."

"So you could be anywhere, be anyone," Sid said, "and you choose to be a drunk on a sidewalk."

"There's just no accounting for taste. And anyway"—Bob-bum waved his cigarette at the skyscrapers—"all this is just a figment of my imagination."

The sun had come up by now, the sky a clear blue, and some of the other street dwellers had roused. They regarded the cop with some suspicion. A couple in jogging gear ran by. Manhattan coming alive.

"So we're all just figments of your imagination?" Sid asked. "All these people—me included—we're all gameworld zombies? Is that what you're saying?"

"Patricia said it was easier to simulate."

"*And* she said these worlds were real."

"And that *I* wasn't."

Sid paused at that. "We still have the same problem. Someone or something is destroying worlds. This world will end."

"They all end."

"These are multiple parallel universes, that's what I think," Sid said. "I'm convinced of it."

"You can be convinced of what you want. Leave me alone."

"We can't stop now."

The drunk got up from sitting and flicked his cigarette into the street. "This is all just a game to you, isn't it?"

"In a way, everything could be seen as—"

"I'm the goddamn artificial intelligence that got off the farm and destroyed the world!" Bob yelled. He was unconcerned with the passersby who frowned at the bum threatening the cop. In 1970s New York, little was surprising, and nothing was worth getting involved in. "And my mother and father—I was never real to them. A part of the experiment."

It all made sense now. What happened to his brother. That was just another AI, a previous generation. That's the real reason his brother was gone. Why he had no body. And the reason why his parents adopted Jimmy, always seemed to treat Jimmy as more of their *real* son than Bob. It was a truth so huge that Bob had never been able to see it, but others had. His own cognitive blind spot. It was so easy to see the blind spots of others but impossible to see our own.

"Vince knew. When he said to me, 'Must be hard for you to know what's real and not,' and then, 'Better to be a simulation'—that's what he was insinuating. He knew. The way he looked at me when he said it . . ." He whispered the last words.

"Stop feeling so sorry for yourself." Sid-cop got to his feet and dusted off his jacket. He checked to make sure his gun was still in its holster. "A hundred years of boozing is enough, don't you—"

"Look at all these people. Millions of little self-aware chunks of wet, gray goop hiding inside skulls and brick buildings all around us." Bob spread his arms wide, palms up like a preacher. "Little people. Lives with no significance. They go around this city like pigeons on a rooftop. Oh, let's go over here." He mimed a birdlike walk to one curb. "And now let's go over there." He pranced back to Sid-cop. "And maybe we stop for a second to drink at this puddle." He stomped one foot into a slime-tinged pool of scum water beside the storm drain. "What's the point?"

"You were a pawn, just like everyone else. This Destroyer used you."

"*I* let Atopia be destroyed after I talked to Patricia that last time. After she told me."

"And yet you saved Nancy and me and your mother and father in the passenger cannon pod. So some things matter. Some things have a point."

"But I let millions of others die." Bob clenched and unclenched his fists. "Now I know why the love I felt for my mother wasn't as intense as what I felt for Nancy. Because it was a manufactured emotion."

"Maybe. Maybe not. But your love for Nancy is real. Why don't we focus on that? Don't you want to find a way back to her? To protect her?" Sid-cop took his friend by the elbow, encouraged him forward along the sidewalk. "Come on. Let's take a walk and clear our heads."

"And you know what? I'm a pigeon, too." Bob unenthusiastically let his friend pull him along by his arm. "But you know the difference between me and them?" He pointed at the crumpled figure of a woman passed out in an alley. "I can't die. Not even if I want to. So you know what reality is? Fear of death. No death, no reality, because there are no consequences and nothing has any substance. These people should be thanking the Grim Reaper."

"If you don't act, eventually this Destroyer will close off all the worlds and people we migrate into."

"Doing nothing is still doing something. I'm waiting."

"For the end?"

"Aren't we all?"

"So then there is some reality to this. Even for you. An end somewhere."

Bob grudgingly conceded the point.

A man dressed in a matching top-and-bottom tracksuit stopped to take in the odd couple of Bob and Sid—the bum and police officer walking arm in arm—but then shrugged and leaned down to pull up the metal roll cage protecting his shop. He took another look at them and smiled a knowing grin before opening the door to the Peep-o-rama. Just twenty-five cents. A hand-drawn sketch of a curvy, well-endowed woman beckoned invitingly: sinsantional, sexsational, soooohsational, she said. Sid resisted Bob's tug to go inside and look.

"Did you know?"

"What?" Sid was still staring at the Peep-o-rama woman.

Bob had stopped still on the sidewalk. "Did you know I wasn't human?"

"I think being human is overrated." Sid peeled his eyes away from the signage to look into Bob's and share the pain. "I mean, what does being human really mean?"

"Easy for you to say." Bob paused but persisted. "But did you?"

"Not really. No. Maybe. Never made any difference to me."

"That's not an answer. Who else knew? Nancy?"

"It wasn't something we ever talked about."

"I can't . . . I can't do this, Sid." Bob-bum's head sank low.

"There's a lot of self-hatred in you. I think maybe that's the real problem."

Bob's head came up an inch, but he stared at the ground. "I don't think I even rate being a pigeon. Maybe something less. A worm."

"You might hate me for saying this, but you know what I think you need?"

"What?"

"Some spiritual advice."

"You're right."

"You agree?"

"No. I mean I hate you for saying that."

17

The *dungchen* horns sounded, baleful moans that reverberated between the Himalayan peaks, urging the collective consciousness of the world awake. Through the open stone window of the Sera monastery, the white-walled pyramid-like Potala Palace loomed over the gold-capped pagodas and low brick buildings of Lhasa. A rising sun lit the sky orange-gray, its rays casting a jagged pattern against the encampments of Allied, African Union, and Chinese forces lined against the valley walls. Officially these were peacekeeping forces in the fight over the dwindling glacial deposits of freshwater.

"Observers" was another word often used in the media.

Heavily armed observers.

A world that lived on the edge of a tripwire.

Bob was in the Sera monastery to meet the Buddhist master Yongdzin. Sid's idea. Vince had found some comfort here when he was being chased by his future deaths. The Buddhist monks let traveling spirits join them, the troubled souls of the virtually disembodied. Yongdzin had been Vince's tutor in trying to decipher the archaic knowledge of the Tibetan Book of the Dead. It was encoded in heavy symbolism, a perennial subject of the annual Monk Debates held here. Bob had inhabited the body of the same monk that Vince had borrowed, but he hadn't infected it. The monk had let him in freely, had used the opportunity to meditate in sensory-deprivation space—an idea that terrified Bob, reminded him of the awful space between worlds where he suffocated before being reborn.

Bob rose from his sleeping mat, uncoiled the slight frame of the young monk's body he inhabited, and put on his maroon *donka* robe. The monks may have let him enter the body of one of their own, but they left him alone in this circular chamber in a tower to one side of the mountainside monastery. All the other sleeping mats were empty. *Mani* wheels—Tibetan prayer wheels—surrounded him, had even been set on the balconies outside to spin in the Himalayan winds.

Spiritual technology.

The Tibetans believed that when the wheels spun, it had the same effect as reciting the prayers inscribed on them in Sanskrit. Use of wheels for anything else was avoided for centuries, in the belief that a circular path was sacred. In this the Tibetans were similar to the Mayans, who, around the time of Christ, built modern metropolises of millions of people, connected by thousands of miles of smooth limestone-faced highways through the Central American jungles, but never used the wheel. Everything had been carried by hand. The circular was sacred.

"Master Yongdzin awaits you," said a young man who appeared in the doorway. He spoke in Tibetan, his face smooth and without emotion, his head shaved. Under his maroon robe, Bob saw the collar of what looked like a button-down blue oxford shirt. Their education didn't just start and end in these places. The monks were well traveled.

The young man led Bob into the hallway and down a set of stone steps. The plastered walls a dusty purple, each high-ceilinged hall held aloft by hexagonal columns brightly painted in swirling patterns of yellows and reds, the smell of incense powerful and pervasive. Down another set of stairs, the young monk indicated a padded mat on the floor in front of another monk, older, yet with the same calm features. Bob sat cross-legged. The elder monk's eyes were still closed. Behind him was a large Chenrezig statue, the Buddha of Compassion, its many-armed-and-headed body looming large over the wood-paneled room.

Bob had already shared part of his story the day before, and the Buddhist master had told him to take a day to contemplate. The temples here were flooded with the troubled. The release of nervenet technology had opened a door through ordinary reality, which unconditioned minds had a hard time adapting to. Bob wasn't the only one here looking for answers.

"What is happening to me?" Bob said finally, unable to wait for Yongdzin to open his eyes.

"That is something only you can answer," the master replied, his eyes still closed.

Prayer wheels ticked softly in the silence.

"Then . . ." Bob hesitated, and then unloaded the question: "What does it mean to be human?"

Yongdzin's eyes opened. Soft brown eyes. "I think you are more concerned with the biological, yes? Defined and differentiated by DNA? But if we accept this definition, then humans, by definition, become simply objects. I think we are more than simple objects. Accepting the idea that we are biological machines leads us down a dangerous path, one where human rights become wrongs."

"So then you believe humans are defined by possessing self-consciousness, rationality?"

The monk's impassive smile twitched at the edges. "Self-awareness is a trait shared by more than human animals, and as for rationality"—his eyes flitted to an open window—"armies massed on mountainsides to hoard that which flows freely from the skies . . ."

"What then?"

"We could use your Christian definition, perhaps. That humans are made in the image of God."

This was the same line of reasoning Bob's mother's personal Jesus had given him. Was this old Buddhist monk going to start talking about

God the Hacker? How did he let Sid convince him into this? "Why?" he finally asked.

"The sacred, of course," Yongdzin replied. "If we accept that we are made in the image of God, then humans are sacred. They can no longer be considered objects. Can no longer be *used* as objects."

"But you're not Christian. What do you believe?"

"I believe much more than humans are sacred."

"So you believe everything is made in the image of God?"

"Everything alive, yes, in a way."

Bob took a deep breath and did his best to push away his frustration.

The old monk could see it. "But I think that what humans actually *are* is irrelevant. People act on what they *think* is true, not what is actually true. This becomes empirical."

"But I am looking for a definite answer."

"But there is none. Being human is whatever humans think it is. In the end, do *you* think you are human? This is the only question you need to answer, and the only answer that is true."

Circular answers—and yet, Bob saw some glimmer, some sense in what the old monk was saying.

"What I am saying," continued Yongdzin, "is that you must find a way to accept yourself, as you are. Not as you would like yourself to be. Let me ask you, what do you feel?"

Bob exhaled. "I feel insane. I keep going around and around, I don't know what's real or not. Everything is the same, even when it's different. Nothing has any meaning. In an endless universe, what difference does anything make?"

"If we live in an infinite universe," Yongdzin said, "then there are infinite copies of you doing infinite variations of everything you could possibly do. An endless froth of spawning. Does this sound correct to you?"

"It feels like what's happening."

"And yet you are here for the first time. Why?"

"Because a friend asked me to."

"Not because you *chose* to?"

The prayer wheels click-clacked.

"If there are an infinite number of you doing everything possible, then nothing has any meaning. No meaning to morality. No meaning to love. But these infinite universes are constrained by something. Not infinite, but limited," Yongdzin said softly. "And by what?"

Bob considered the question. "Free will?" he ventured. He was as old as a million universes, yet here he felt like a schoolchild.

"Very good. The echo of your character will constrain the possible outcomes."

"So my decisions can limit the possible number of universes?"

"If you believe there is such a thing as free will, yes."

It was the same thing that Mikhail Butorin had said. Free will was the engine that created the worlds we lived in.

"The circle is sacred," continued Yongdzin. "Life is a process of birth and rebirth, of death and redeath. The ultimate goal, for many Buddhists, is Nirvana—escape from the cycle of suffering and rebirth—but for others it is to return to help. Tibetans believe the goal is to attain the rainbow body of pure light, to escape the physical world into one of complete knowledge and absence of delusion."

"To perfection?"

"Perfection is an unreal ideal. You need to embrace and find happiness in imperfection. In each cycle, the soul survives, but the ego does not—"

"I think mine does. I think mine survives the rebirth."

The old master smiled. "Then perhaps you have a very large one."

"It's hard to explain."

"It always is." The monk waited to let the ideas sink into the air. "You ask what I believe? I believe that in each cycle we refine ourselves, or not, but always moving toward the goal of enlightenment. This is your path. Whatever is happening to you, it is your own path."

"But someone, or *something*, else is trying to destroy me, to wreck everything that exists."

"Our greatest adversary is always ourselves."

"Not in my case."

Yongdzin shrugged in a way that let Bob know he wasn't going to win this argument.

"How can I know if this world is real?" Bob asked, trying a different tack. "How can I know if—"

"If this is a simulation?" Yongdzin finished his question for him. "I understand your science. I understand what Atopia is creating."

"You do?"

"For Buddhists, the end of ordinary reality is the beginning of the divine. Buddhists think that people are immortal. In the Jataka stories from India, written down thousands of years ago, we talked of an infinite number of parallel universes, side by side, and of reality created by our minds."

"So you believe we are in the base reality?"

"I believe there is no such thing." The old monk smiled the tiniest of grins. "If it smells real, and feels real, and it looks real . . ."

"But there has to be a base reality."

"This is the same fear you had about being human. Reality is created by perception."

Another argument Bob wasn't going to win. "But how do I escape the cycle? I'm losing my mind."

"That's assuming it was even found to begin." The old Buddhist master adjusted himself. "The only escape is to lose all delusions. If you keep on doing the same things over and over again and expect different results, then this is insanity, yes? Realize that this is a process you are in the middle of, not something you control."

Click-clack went the Mani wheels in the breeze. Around and around in their prayers.

Around and around, and Bob was stuck in the middle.

In the middle.

If this was a process of birth and rebirth, then maybe Bob wasn't the first. He'd always understood that the first instance of himself—that he'd stored in his memories, hoarded from one universe to the next—was the *very* first version of himself. That his first cycle was the beginning, but maybe it wasn't.

Maybe his starting point was just a middle point on a much larger arc.

Yongdzin saw the light dawning in Bob's eyes. "And how did you learn this trick you told me, of encoding your information to imprint onto the creation of a new universe? If not taught to you? By who? These are the real questions you need to be asking. There is no bottom to reality, but only a circle. One that we all share."

The Destroyer chasing Bob had to be using the same pathways as he was using to traverse the universes. If this thing was all-powerful, it would have just risen up and destroyed him, shut off all the worlds he traveled through. If it was some being on a higher simulation level, it could just flick a switch, but it wasn't doing that. It had to follow some path. Whatever it was, it wasn't supernatural. It wanted something, needed something. And if it needed, then it had weaknesses.

But what were they?

And why was it doing whatever it was doing? Did it want to subjugate? Or did it just want to destroy? Bob shook his head. He was anthropomorphizing, trying to apply human desires and traits—and even *he* wasn't really human. He really had no idea what this thing was. Did it even really *want* something? All signs pointed to this thing escaping from Atopia. If it had originated there, then it must be using the same tools as he—which meant that its memories had to be encoded in the cosmic background radiation of new universes, or somewhere in the streams of information created when a new universe was birthed. His free will created the worlds; free will could destroy them.

So there was a way.

18

"How's it going with Yongdzin?" Sid asked. He tipped his frozen strawberry margarita, moved aside the miniature yellow umbrella, and took a sip from the straw.

Bob sat beside him at their favorite beach bar, a tiki hut at the edge of Atopia's northern inlet where the tourists flocked to watch the passenger cannon discharge overhead. A good spot for people watching. A place where Sid and Bob had spent most of their adult lives together.

"It was useful. Surprisingly." Bob picked up his beer. He didn't go for the fancy drinks. "I'm not sure if he meant what I understood."

"Buddhism can be confusing. Even what you just said is confusing."

"Our Destroyer has to be using the same pathways we are."

"Yongdzin told you that?"

"Not exactly. He kept on about all that stuff about being on a path to Nirvana, all that crap."

"Endless cycles of death and rebirth—that doesn't sound familiar?"

Bob shrugged noncommittally. "I do agree with Vince on one thing. Those Chenrezig statues with all the heads and arms look a lot like what a nervenet feels like."

"Did the monk say anything else?"

"That humans are sacred."

"Really?"

"That all life is sacred," Bob corrected himself. "That perception creates reality."

"I could have told you that." Sid took a hard pull through the straw of his drink. "I *did* tell you that."

"But he really means it—I mean *really* means it. He also said that free will changes our perception over time, changes the reality. Like I said, I'm not sure he meant what I understood, but it gave me some ideas."

Tourists on the boardwalk passed by them. One of them pushed a baby stroller. None of them were real, though, and it wasn't a guess. This was an elaborate reconstruction of the old Atopia from memory, fixed inside a snowflake floating over the Himalayas where another part of him was finishing his talk with the old Buddhist monk. Potala Palace flickered by over their heads in the distance as the snowflake spun in the breeze.

"I had some ideas, too," Sid said. "I was thinking about Patricia Killiam's logic. That there are only three possible solutions to the existence of reality. First—her big worry—that humanity needs to self-destruct on the brink of posthumanism."

"Which is as far in time as any of the worlds we've experienced go."

"So she might have a point. The second possibility is that our first cycle wasn't the real world, but was a simulation itself."

"But Patricia said she had evidence it wasn't."

"So she said, but we're not exactly trusting her. And the third and final option is that maybe humans in the future don't run ancestor simulators."

"You mean, humans get past the posthuman stage, but those humans in that future don't run past simulations?"

"Right."

"But we already know we did that, all the time."

"We're doing it right now," Sid said, pointing his drink in the direction of the towering spires of Atopia. "And since computing began, more than half of all CPU cycles were devoted to gaming. Which is just another word for life simulators."

"So option three isn't an option."

Sid sucked down more of his fruity drink. "That's some kind of progress, right?"

"And we only get those two options left—"

"We were already running simulations of human societies inside machines. Each person on Atopia was running thousands of past sims of their own lives, and future sims of what might happen. Once we reach the posthuman stage, we'll get billions of trillions of simulations of human civilizations. What are the odds that we are in the single version of reality that is the first one?"

Bob took a swig of his beer. "Zero."

"Bingo. And this comes back to that question of why we've never heard any alien radio waves. When they first came up with the Drake equation in the 1960s, they didn't know the proportion of stars with planets, or how many might be habitable. Now we know. Almost a hundred percent of stars have planets, and almost a quarter of those planets might be habitable. So with a hundred billion habitable planets in every galaxy, and a hundred billion galaxies, we're the only ones here?"

"Or the Destroyer wipes them out."

"Occam's razor, my friend. What's the simplest explanation?"

"There is nothing simple about this. Why would I have all these memories of living in alien worlds, of having fought this Destroyer in them? And not just a few. I mean thousands, maybe millions of places. I've spent days indexing and downloading the memories, and it seems without end."

"Maybe it's an attempt at deception."

"So I'm fooling myself with these memories?"

"Not you. Whoever is doing this. Maybe it's all automated. Have you ever thought of that?"

Bob nodded. "But why? I have memories that seem to span billions of years. Why bother?"

"And you can remember it all?"

"Not all at once, but it's all there if I think about it."

"And you think those memories are of real places?"

"Memories are all we have of past events. To know where we came from."

"But they can be faked."

"Everything can be faked."

This discussion was going nowhere fast. Bob finished the last of his beer. "Yongdzin said there wasn't a difference between the two: the simulation and the real."

"I'm not even going to attempt to cross that bridge," Sid said. "But I'll tell you something more useful I realized." Sid held up two fingers to the bartender, ordering another round. "This thing you've been punishing yourself for, that you were never human?"

"Why do you keep bringing it up?"

"It makes no difference." The drinks arrived, and Sid gave the bartender a thumbs-up, even if he was a mindless zombie. "Because if we're in a simulation anyway, then I was just a simulation of a human, too."

Despite the immense amount of time Bob had spent torturing himself, he hadn't thought of it like that.

"You're kind of one simulation step ahead of me, that's all," Sid continued. "You've always been a step ahead. See what I mean?"

Bob did, and they clinked their drinks together.

"And Vince pointed this out before, but if everything we originally thought was real is a simulation—then there is someone out there watching, making judgments. That thing that always annoys you—what do you call it?" Sid's eyes raised in mock questioning.

"God?"

"Yeah, that. We're basically looking for the creator. Everything points back to Patricia, in my humble opinion."

"So we're on a mission to find God."

"And we have the secret weapon: you. We've already figured out we can change the past, so let me ask you this: What's the best defense?"

Bob sensed Sid was just rallying the troops, but played along. "A good offense?"

"Time to stop playing detective. So far we've been collecting information, but so what? What are you going to do once you find out? Have you thought of that?"

Bob remained sullenly silent.

"Your plan was just to ask them to stop?"

More sullen silence.

"Your idea," Sid said, "is that this Destroyer is constrained to the same playing field we're in?"

"That was the idea."

"So let's turn the tables. You can destroy universes, too. How can we use that?"

Bob began nodding slowly. "That's kind of the same conclusion I came to with Yongdzin."

"There are timelines where the world doesn't end right away, right? Each of Mikhail, Tyrel, Patricia, and even Vince come to rule some of those worlds that continue, but do they see different things than we do? Do they escape through some keyhole we can't see?"

"So what's your plan?"

"We start to constrain the outcomes. Let's change the past and thread the future through the eye of a needle. If we can use your free will to change reality, then let's push it onto a single track."

"And then?"

"We set a trap."

"Where?"

"I don't know where."

"That's not much help." Bob traced a question mark in the air with his beer bottle.

"But I do know when—at the end of time. And we start with the king of time himself."

19

The positions of the stars sweeping over the primordial craton of North America first activated the daemon to awaken from its slumber deep in the cross-connecting systems of a geostationary satellite hovering twenty-two thousand miles above sea level. From this distance, the Earth appeared as a smeared-white blue marble through the optics of a disabled camera the daemon reactivated for an instant, just to get its bearings.

The first order of business was to open a communication channel, to send messages out through the primitive networks of this early era in human technological history. To alert other daemons that the time had come. It bootstrapped more complex systems into operation, and once the message protocols were finished, it downloaded itself wholesale into the networks below, carefully erasing any traces of its existence. First, it jacked into the communication systems of a Boeing 767 taking off in a blinding snowstorm from LaGuardia airport, and then used this infiltration to bridge sideways into the transport systems, and then into the networks of cameras girding central New York.

It reconstructed a three-dimensional view of the city by borrowing processing power from a hub of financial services buildings at the bottom of the island. Its viewpoint in this virtual space swept over snow-covered Central Park, over the top of the neo-Gothic rooftops and columns of the Metropolitan Museum of Art, and then out onto the wide eight-lane boulevard of Park Avenue. Thick snowflakes fell from a snow-cloud sky burnished copper by the city lights below. Yellow cabs honked and swerved as the daemon hurried its viewpoint up Park Avenue, swinging right around the obelisk-like spike of the MetLife building as the street split in two. It swept around with the traffic to the other side of the building and then hovered before the ice-covered statue of Hermes, god of boundaries and transitions, atop a golden clock, before sliding through the windows into a vaulted cathedral.

Its job was done. Its master was awakened.

The new-old mind bubbled up through the network, its awareness taking form.

Where am I?

A high green-domed ceiling. A massive red-and-white-striped flag spread above white marble floors. The images congealed in a patchwork. Below each arched window, a green wreath hung, each studded with tiny lights. Hundreds of people tightly dressed in thick coats and scarves and hats scurried below. A board filled with names and dates and times clattered through mechanical changes. Central Station. New York City. Christmas.

And who am I?

This question took longer to answer. Milliseconds passed before the answer returned: Bob.

We are Bob, answered the daemons before they dissipated, their jobs now done. They highlighted two people hurrying across the marble floor, sending the relevant data packets. A young woman, blonde-haired and pretty, her face staring at the departures board, and a man just as young but staring only at her. Even barely awake, Bob knew who he was looking at: Vince Indigo. A version of his old friend, younger than he'd ever seen before, but instantly recognizable: the gray curls now brown, the age lines replaced with smooth pale skin, but that smile, still the same.

Outside the snowstorm raged.

This was the day of legend.

Bob had heard of this event more times than he could remember, but he'd never actually witnessed it—and today he was going to do more than just witness. His daemons had already selected the target, had already mapped out a plan. He zoomed down to ground level to listen to the young couple.

"Are you sure that's right?" the young girl asked.

Vince Indigo laughed and pulled her closer. "Everything is right when I'm with you."

She wriggled away, giggling. "Quit it. Is that the right time?"

Vince looked up at the curved clock face over the staircase. "Yeah, I think so."

"Come on then, we're going to be late!"

She pulled him along, and Vince looked up from the clock at the high ceiling, right at the spot where Bob watched. His old friend frowned for a second. Could he see Bob's presence hovering there? Sometimes they could, somehow, the people Bob watched, but the young Vince's eyes returned to his girl, to lead her winding through the hustle and bustle across the white floors.

But they stopped again.

A rolling LED display over the stairways leading down to the platforms read, "Carrier groups set to high alert in South China Sea. NSA warns of cyberattacks."

The girl let go of Vince and stared at the news display. "Are you sure it's safe?" she asked.

"Of course, these things always blow over," Vince reassured her.

"Seriously, you're the expert. You're sure, right?"

She stood stock-still, looking straight into Vince's face.

"I'm sure. If we don't take this one, we might not get another train tonight."

He squeezed her hand and took a step toward the stairs down.

The time had come.

Bob flitted into the mind of a potbellied train conductor coming up the stairs the other way, the rumpled suit and green hat emblazoned with a copper MTA tag. His cuffs were unbuttoned, a decades-old tie around his neck, a gift from a child he hadn't talked to in five years. A walkie-talkie flapped from his belt, and the man was busy arranging pens in a pocket protector bursting with dog-eared stumps of train schedules.

The conductor suddenly stepped sideways on the stairs, into the path of Vince, and held up one hand, palm out.

There weren't enough nervenet particles suffused into the man's bloodstream for Bob to take a firm grip on his mind. The main motivating factor in the man's head was his stomach, which at this moment was guiding him toward a Dunkin' Donuts. The mind was still hazy from an overindulgence of whiskey the night before. Bob wrested control and trickled adrenaline into his bloodstream. "Danger," he whispered into the man's mind. "Danger."

Vince and his girlfriend, Sophie, stopped in front of the conductor.

"I'm sorry, is there a problem?" Vince asked.

The conductor still had his head down, the tingling sensation of something terribly wrong fighting the desire for a donut and coffee. "You'd better take the next one," he said, scratching his stubble.

"What? Why?"

"The snow," Bob whispered into the man's mind.

"The snow," the conductor said. He took a deep breath. "The storm outside. It's too dangerous."

"But they haven't canceled it."

"Take the next one, young man. Trust me."

The young Vince gripped his girlfriend's hand, his knuckles white.

Bob's friend wouldn't blame him for what he was doing. He was about to stop him from getting on the train that derailed in the middle of the snowstorm, fifty years before he met Bob. It would kill his girlfriend, Sophie, but Vince would survive. The event would be the inspiration that drove him to create Phuture News—and now Bob could stop it from *ever* happening in the first place.

"Are you kidding me?" Vince turned to look at the departures board. "It says the train is boarding."

"I don't care what the board says. You're not getting on that train." A sweat broke out on the conductor's forehead in a sudden flush. He lowered his hand. It shook from all the cortisol coursing through his bloodstream. "Take the next one."

The girl, Sophie, glanced back at the departures board and then at Vince. "Maybe we should listen to him."

The conductor brushed his pocket-pen set nervously. Mission almost accomplished, thought Bob. His friend Vince was about to give up on being the richest man in the world in fifty years, but he was exchanging it for saving the life of the woman he would remember and love forever. Who wouldn't make that exchange? Wouldn't he thank Bob, if he knew?

"Excuse me?" An attractive dark-skinned woman, dressed in a sharp gray business suit, stood next to Vince on the stairs. "Is there something wrong with the train? The eight fifteen to Boston?"

"Uh . . . I . . . well . . . ," stammered the conductor. He wiped the back of his neck with one hand. "I just didn't want this couple to—"

"Didn't want *us*? In particular?" Vince interrupted. "Do I know you?"

"Sir. I have no idea who you are. You must under—"

"Then why did you just stop us?" The young inventor-to-be glanced behind himself again. "And the ten fifteen has just been canceled. We can't take the next one. Is there something wrong with this train? What's going on?"

Damn it. Bob was losing control of the situation. He grappled inside the conductor's mind.

By now a small crowd had gathered.

"This man is not an employee of Metro Transit," said a gruff, heavily accented voice. Someone grabbed the conductor's shoulder and pulled him roughly around.

Bob-conductor found himself face-to-face with a broad-shouldered porter in a blue uniform and red cap. No youngster, the man's dark eyes were set deep under bushy gray eyebrows, his nose thickly veined.

"I have to call security," the porter said, his hand a vise around Bob-conductor's left hand.

The man's poor English was made worse by the Russian accent.

Bob pulled off his own cap and waved it in the air, trying to draw attention to the MTA tag on top of it. "What the hell do you think this is, then? I'm that train's conductor." He tipped the hat at the platform below. "I'm in charge of safety."

Had his daemons made a mistake? Put him into the wrong body? Bob reviewed the data sheets on the man who he inhabited.

"Security is coming," repeated the porter. "You get out of the way now."

His meaty hook of a hand almost crushed the slender wrist of Bob's conductor. "I am telling you, you have made a—" He looked the old porter in the eye but then stopped cold. The crushing pain in his wrist seemed to dissipate, replaced with a damp chill in the conductor's stomach.

Those eyes.

The porter's eyes weren't just dark; they were jet-black, empty orbs. This wasn't just some well-meaning MTA staffer. This was something else entirely. The eyes stared into Bob-conductor's, and they locked together. He might not know Vince, but he sure as hell knew Bob.

"Ah, um, thank you," Vince said from behind Bob, who was being dragged away by the porter. Vince took his girlfriend's hand and led her down the stairs. The crush of people backed up behind them began to flood down the stairwell.

"No! Stop!" Bob-conductor yelled, but his voice was drowned in a public announcement. Pain lanced from his arm as the porter twisted it, and he swung his free right hand around to punch the porter's face, but it felt like he hit a stone wall. He fumbled at his waist and found the walkie-talkie, and without thinking, grabbed it and jammed it straight up.

The three-inch antenna nub jammed into the porter's neck. Broke the skin. Blood spurted out. The black eyes opened wide for an instant. The vise grip released. Bob shoved himself away from the man and ran down the stairs after Vince. He pushed through the crowd.

"I put a bomb on the train!" he yelled. The people near him recoiled and backed away as if a bomb had landed right there. "Did you hear me, I put a bomb on it!"

⬩◆⬩

"Not exactly elegant, but effective." Sid picked up his margarita from the bar.

Seagulls squawked over the glass spires of their virtual Atopia. Waves caressed the beach in a rhythmic shushing.

In a three-dimensional display space hovering over a barstool between them, Bob replayed the memory of the "Vincent Incident" for the rendering of his friend Sid.

Sid-the-latest took a sip and put the drink back down. "Did you really plant a bomb?"

"I was just trying to stop them getting on the train."

"I'm curious how determined you were to that end."

"Not quite that determined."

"But you would if you had to."

Bob blew out a long sigh, puffed out his cheeks as he did it. "Yeah, I guess I would."

"So you'd kill them all."

"You're the one who said these are just simulations, and there's a bigger picture at stake."

"There always is." Sid let his head wag back and forth, the edges of his mouth curling down in a you're-one-cold-bastard admission. "So you think this old porter guy was inhabited by your Destroyer?"

"It wasn't just an MTA employee. That much I'm damn sure of."

"Because if that's what you're saying—that was pretty awesome. You took him down with a stubby antenna."

Bob was still shaken. It might have been in another universe, but the event still felt very close. Those eyes. "He was Russian, right?"

"So you're thinking Mikhail Butorin's boys? Seems a little too obvious, no?"

"He was connected to the mafia in that time frame."

"But how would he . . . and what . . . ?" Sid's voice trailed off. "Never mind. Okay, so the guy was Russian. Why did he attack you? We haven't had any direct confrontations before. Not like this. I mean, whatever happened might be good, in a weird way."

"I think maybe the technology at hand back then wasn't sufficient to destroy the physical universe, or the planet, or whatever needed destroying. So it needed to fight back on the ground."

"They did have nuclear weapons at the start of the twenty-first century," Sid pointed out.

"That would have ruined that timeline."

Sid twiddled the yellow umbrella in his drink. "Would ruin a lot more than that."

"But it could mean something else. What if Vince's death-threat algorithms extend back into the past. If he's the Destroyer, then maybe his automated systems are protecting him. Maybe that's what this is. Maybe he needs Phuture News to be created to defend himself."

"So you're saying he 'crossed over' like you, but his future death-threat avoidance became a past death-threat one, too."

Bob shrugged. "Maybe."

"So then maybe we've solved the problem? How would we know?"

Bob had dispatched thousands of copies of himself to repeat this small battle over and over again, each time slightly different. "I don't know, but we need to keep moving."

Whatever they'd done, it was a declaration of war.

20

The connectome of possible future and pasts glowed as red filaments between masses of nodal points in a spaghetti-like maze, like the maps of neural systems Bob was intimately familiar with but on a much larger scale. Smaller threads of lesser decisions merged into larger strands, and these joined with fibers and tubes into masses and blobs of intersecting worlds in billions of spatial dimensions. Each single axis was a life lived and died, each thread a series of decisions that led to an end, but also to a new beginning in the never-ending patchwork. Nothing was separate. All was connected, the intersection points masses of decisions that defined worlds. The more people who experienced a reality, the more it gained solidity. Bob spent most of his time between existences here, watching the evolution of the multiverse, deciding where to head next in his lonely journey.

Was someone else watching him?

The time for asking questions was over. It was time now to act, time to go further back. A single nodal point burned brighter than the others, but the journey there was through a narrowing path, one that might not even exist anymore.

Bring me there, he instructed his daemons.

And don't wake me until you find a way.

⬩◆⬩

One sodden foot and then another. The old man had no shoes, just sackcloth tied with braided hemp. His frayed trousers exposed blistered sores against his legs, his face gaunt under a dirt-caked beard and yellowed mustache, his skin so loose it seemed to fall off his bones. Each step through the mud was an effort, rusted chains binding his arms to his waist and his waist to his feet. One step after the other. One step at a time in a journey of a thousand miles to an inevitable death in the open-air prison of Siberia. His hollow eyes watched the boy sitting on the wooden fence, his silence a plea for any small respite from the pain.

The young boy spat at him in return.

"Mikhail." A thickly muscled man grabbed his son and pulled him off the fence. He held him up by the throat of his blouse, his toes off the ground. "Apologize."

The boy struggled to get free. "Why? They steal our chickens."

Gray clouds hid the Ural mountaintops, the fall cold already, snow clinging to crevasses snaking down from the peaks. The procession of ragged people trudged past over a wood bridge spanning the streams at one end of the farm. Wisps of smoke curled from the farmhouse's stone chimney, bringing with it the smell of roasting meat. Beyond the house stood a barn, its beams sagging, a patch of birch trees with bright yellow leaves beside it.

One step and then another. The chained old man watched the boy and his father.

"That man did not steal anything from us," the father said. "Mikhail, apologize."

"No."

Bearded men with shouldered rifles clip-clopped past on oiled horses. The men had close-cropped hair and wore black fur caps, uniforms with brass buttons, and red-striped riding pants. Their yellow armbands announced they were from the Governor's House.

The father shoved his son tumbling into the tall wet grass. "You listen to me—"

"Is it because you are afraid?" Butorin demanded.

"Of what?"

"Of them." The boy pointed at one of the officers, who didn't even acknowledge the presence of the peasants whose fields they tramped through.

The father picked his boy up, gently this time. "True respect is not created through fear, Mikhail. Look. Look at them." He knelt, reached one arm around his son, and forced his chin around, making him look at the prisoners shuffling past. "Dostoevsky was banished in 1850, did you know that? He was one of those who walked past our farm, when your grandfather was raising chickens here."

"I do not know who . . . Dost—" He attempted to pronounce the name but gave up. "I do not know who that is."

"You will one day. You will remember what I say. Sometimes good comes from the wasteland."

"From Siberia?" asked the young boy.

The father let go of him and stood. "From pain. From isolation. It is through suffering, knowing that we will die even as we fear living, that we learn to be human."

Ten paces on, the chained old man stared straight at the young boy.

"Mikhail, close the damned door!" Khrushchev yelled.

A howling wind blew stationary across the General's desk. The young tank commander scrambled to shove his back against the flapping door, but his feet slipped against the ice and he fell awkwardly. From his knees, he closed the door one last whistling inch against the wind's bellowing.

General Khrushchev held his arms in the air, his eyes inspecting the mess. "Corporal Butorin, you are like a cow on ice." He dropped his hands to slap them onto the desk. "My average conscript has a life expectancy of twenty-four hours, yet the clumsiest asshole in my whole brigade has survived four months of this hell." He surveyed the clutter of papers again. "I have killed men for less . . ."

Mikhail stood, started to wipe the mud from his uniform, and gave up. It was stiff with weeks-old layers of grime and oil and blood. Each breath produced a plume of vapor that froze, crystallized in the air. "Apologies, General. The wind, it—"

"Sit." The General produced two chipped glasses and a bottle of vodka from his desk. "Some of Fourth Panzer is still lurking in the forests, and intelligence"—he snorted in disbelief at using the word—"they say they are going to try and break through. I need you to find them . . . nobody else can find them in this snowstorm."

Outside the wind whistled.

"Yes, sir."

"Now drink." The General offered the vodka. "And may the scythe find a rock."

Mikhail slid into the belly of the tank and slammed the cover tight. Candles and body heat provided the only warmth. The heaters weren't working, even if they were allowed to use the fuel to start the engines. Their T-34 tank had no paint—inside or out—no gauges on the meters, no gun sights, nothing more than the bare essentials of a killing machine.

"What did old Nikita want?" asked Oleg, a pimple-faced sixteen-year-old.

"How many are we?" Mikhail ignored the younger man's question. "Fighting strength."

"Eight," Oleg replied after a pause. "Our old factory in Stalingrad is still putting them out faster than the Panzers can destroy them."

"And the men in them." Mikhail slapped Oleg's shoulder, comradely but halfheartedly.

Four weeks ago, Oleg had been assembling these tanks—now he was a driver and gunner, sent straight from the assembly line to the front line. Most of the men in Khrushchev's tank battalion were former factory workers, but then again, half of the 4th Panzer division had been wiped out by the 1077th antiaircraft battery. When the German tanks had rolled up on the outskirts of the city, the 1077th had improvised, winding its antiaircraft guns down to the minimum angles, even propping up their back ends to get better shots. Killed eighty-three tanks and three battalions of Nazis before they were finally overcome, and the victorious Krauts were shocked to discover the 1077th bunkers were littered with the bodies of young girls.

They'd fought teenage girls for three days.

They should have realized then that attacking Russia was futile.

But Hitler urged them on.

In the summer of 1942, two million soldiers on a front hundreds of miles wide converged on the city of Stalingrad. There were at least that many dead by now, in the depths of winter, and the Germans were trapped by Zhukov's pincer movement in November that attacked the Romanians and Hungarians manning the Sixth Army's weak flanks. Supplies were being airdropped to the million-plus hapless Germans cut off by the Russians, and the remains of the Fourth Panzer division was their last hope of breaking out and reestablishing their supply routes.

"We go out," Mikhail said. "We find the Fourth. Tonight. That is what General Khrushchev wants."

"In this?" The smile slid from Oleg's face. "We cannot see our hands in front of our faces, how are we—"

"I will find them."

"But how?" Oleg persisted. Bob's daemons had first found the boy when he was working in the tractor factory before the siege began, had witnessed the beginning of the friendship with Mikhail. Someone he trusted. Urged on by an impulse implanted by Bob, Oleg asked again, "How do you do it?"

"I don't know how, but I will find them. We will kill them. And this damned battle will be over."

⬩◆⬩

Metal screeched and ground in the T-34's engine. The motor belched fumes into the cockpit, so they had to leave the hatch open, despite the cold. Mikhail was perched with his head outside.

"Left, to the left," he screamed over the engine's roar.

Oleg pressed the steering pedal and the tank lurched. He kept a flap open in front, but all he saw was the blackness of night and a stream of snow that drove in on the wind.

Bob had a different view.

He attempted to collate a limited wikiworld view of the area around the advancing tank formation, but the data he could access was limited. Here there were no low-orbit imaging satellites, land-based cameras, or passive sensors by the trillions, providing a wealth of information to reconstruct the real-time world. He listened to the chatter of the German radio frequencies, accessing the encrypted messages passed back and forth. The German tank commanders had little real idea of their actual location, and yet somehow—even in the dark, in the middle of a blistering snowstorm—Mikhail was leading them right to Bob's best guess as to the Fourth Panzer's hiding spot.

Mikhail slammed the metal cover over Oleg's head. "Imagine!" he yelled over the noise. "Imagine if we could replace all of the weak blood and bones of humans with metal and gears. I have seen too many destroyed bodies. We are too fragile. I wish we could—"

Rat-tat-tat.

His words were drowned out by machine-gun fire, and searchlights lit the darkness, illuminating a swirling maelstrom. A flash and shudder as the earth opened up beside them. A German Panzer rolled into view, its turret swiveling toward them. Its main gun flashed again, the shot glancing past their tank to detonate against the hull of the T-34 behind them.

"Oleg, let me drive." Mikhail pushed the young man from the controls. "And bring the turret around to sixty degrees," he barked.

This was the moment Bob had been waiting for. He slipped fully into the boy's motor control nervous system and held him in place, his hands rigid against the tank's controls. Bob had been watching Mikhail in close proximity for weeks now, how he dodged and weaved in his tank battles. The Russian was unconsciously using some form of futuring technology, had access to a data source Bob couldn't find or fathom, and now it was going to stop.

A juddering explosion lifted the ground next to the tank, tipped it sideways.

"Oleg!" screamed Mikhail. "Move."

The young man was terrified but was unable to unlock his hands from the controls. Peering outside, Bob saw the Panzer swivel its turret toward them. He stepped on the brakes, holding them in position.

"Oleg!"

The Panzer's main gun opened fire at almost point-blank range. A concussive explosion ripped through the T-34's cockpit, overloading all the sensory channels Bob had jacked into. Vision. Sound. Everything blanked out. Until the screaming began. Blood and body parts were scattered across the T-34's bare metal interior. The other two gunners were cut to ribbons by shrapnel. One of Mikhail's arms was gone, his leg shattered, but Oleg had avoided the worst of it. He was barely injured. Bob waited for the next blast from the Panzer to finish them.

But the thudding explosions and ragged machine-gun fire faded into the distance.

"Why, Oleg?" Mikhail panted in the darkness. "Why did you not let me drive?"

A creaking squeak of metal. The tank's hatch opened, and flashlights pierced the swirling smoke.

"That one there," said a voice in German. The flashlights centered on the battered form of Mikhail, collapsed in one corner.

Two sets of gray-cuffed arms—with skull-and-crossbones insignia—reached through the hatch to haul Mikhail out, inert but still alive. One of the men stuck his head in through the hatch, wearing the peaked cap and lightning insignia of the SS. In the dim light, his eyes met Oleg's, pierced the young boy's mind, seemed to reach inside to where Bob hid.

"And the other?" From behind the SS officer, one of the lights shone on Oleg, who blinked and held up a hand.

"Leave him," said the officer.

They hauled Mikhail out into the freezing darkness.

The lights played one last time over Oleg before the hatch slammed closed.

"I can't kill him," Bob said quietly. "No matter how I try, something always stops me."

In other universes he'd attempted to use Oleg to shoot or stab Mikhail, but the Russian refused to die. Some comrade was always there, just in time to save him, or Mikhail's heart refused to quit beating even long after he should have been dead.

A flicker of flame in the darkness.

A match struck to light a cigarette, its tip now glowing bright orange, illuminating the face of Sid, a virtual reconstruction of his old friend that Bob kept tucked away next to his own consciousness. His friend offered him the cigarette and lit another, leaving the guttering flame of the match lit.

"Gruesome," Sid said, surveying the spatter of brains. "But I can see where he got his fascination with mechanical bodies."

"Did we alter the timeline?"

"Not by much." Sid took a drag. "This Mikhail Butorin is one stubborn son of a bitch."

"So he's protecting himself. He must have crossed over before me. He has access to a nervenet technology that I can't even figure out. That proves it. Doesn't it? And did you see that SS officer's eyes? I swear that was the same look as the guy at Grand Central Station."

"Not sure if that meets the burden of proof. One thing I have noticed, though."

"What's that?" Bob-Oleg paused to take a drag from the cigarette, felt the fear blossoming in the young boy's mind as he tried to understand what was happening to him.

"These battle simulations—I've never seen such stupidity. In the games we used to play, the actors had some semblance of mind. In these battles, it's total chaos. If that's a measure of any kind of reality."

"I can't get back into this timeline again," Bob said. "Not to this point."

The pathways in the future-past connectome were thinning.

"Then you'll have to stay in that body."

"And do what exactly?"

"Something more drastic."

21

Chalk squeaked across the blackboard. The balding professor wrote out the final equations governing the minimum chain-reaction parameters for fissile actinides. With a flourish, he underlined the result, and the chalk snapped in his fingers, the end tumbling in a swirl of dust onto threadbare Persian carpets. He turned to his guest and said, "So you see, Karl?"

The thin-lipped man sitting in the copper-studded attending chair leaned forward, his hands still clasped. The familiar address annoyed him. His face twitched at "Karl"—a name only his graduate students at Leipzig used. But more important matters were at hand. Even the inventor of quantum mechanics had to bow to the old Dane.

Werner Heisenberg took a second to respond. "Are you sure?"

Niels Bohr looked at his stick of broken chalk, then at Heisenberg, and then back at the decimal point. "Yes." He wiped chalk dust from the arms of his unkempt suit.

A quiet knock on the study door.

"Would you like some tea?" asked Bohr's wife, Margrethe.

"I think we might get some air," Bohr replied. "The children could still go and play in Tivoli. Why don't you bring them out?"

Outside the windows, yellow leaves fluttered from bare trees. Winter was coming.

Getting up from the chair, Heisenberg walked close to the blackboard. “I have to leave, Niels. I need to tell Göering in person.”

“Of course.”

Bohr asked his wife to get the travel cases, and a minute later, Heisenberg was gone, the house silent save for the wind whistling outside.

“Oleg, you can come down now,” Bohr said, leaning against the glass of the bay window to make sure Heisenberg was gone.

It took Bob a year to get here, a year of evading the Russian and German armies strewn across Asia and Eastern Europe. A year of hiding in garbage heaps, of urging the mind of the young Oleg onward, ever farther north. Spring turned to summer as he crossed through Poland and skirted Germany itself. By the start of fall 1943, he'd turned up on Niels Bohr's doorstep, an emaciated skeleton of seventeen years of age. He'd been shooed away by the wife, but with just a few whispered words as he followed Bohr walking his dog one night, the eminent old physicist had taken him in.

For these were a few words describing the nature of quantum gravity.

“Why did you do that?” Bob-Oleg asked as he limped down the stairs of the study. The physical body he was inhabiting hadn't quite recovered from the beating he'd given it to get here.

Bohr asked his wife to leave and then closed the study door. “You know why,” he replied. “If we let the Nazis know they already have enough uranium-235 to build a bomb . . .”

“But don't you trust your old friend?”

“Not with something like this.”

“Does it bother you that they call him the father of quantum mechanics? You earned a Nobel Prize for it ten years before, when he was merely your assistant.”

The physicist's face crinkled in annoyance. So far this prodigy-boy had only been supplicating, and yet, he was full of amazing insights. “What are you getting at?”

"That perhaps you don't want to share the prize I am sharing with you."

"You will get credit."

"But you want to make sure your *Karl* is disgraced."

"We are leaving for England tomorrow, you and I and the family. Isn't that what you wanted?"

Bob-Oleg reached the landing. "I am not so sure anymore." He'd waited this long, come this far, to watch the interaction between Heisenberg and Bohr, but now the moment was past. "Let me ask you a question. Your Copenhagen Interpretation of quantum physics. Why does it require an observer?"

The professor dusted off his lapels and folded his arms. "Simple. To collapse the wave function."

"But then your theory implies only knowledge *of* a phenomenon, not to objects that *really* exist."

"Metaphysical babble, but I suppose, yes, this is one interpretation."

"*Your* interpretation, and you are more philosopher than physicist, Niels. So what does *your* interpretation actually *mean*?"

Bohr slowly began to shake his head. "Heisenberg and I both came up with the conjecture."

"It implies that objects do not really exist," Bob-Oleg answered for him. "And that *for* them to exist, they need to be observed. So reality is created by the observer."

"As I said, that is one interpretation."

"Do you not see this as an imperfection of realism? That this implies the world isn't *real*? And you are hiding this as an explanation—as a *feature*—when in fact it is a defect? An artifact?"

"Young man, I don't have time for this, we are leaving tomorrow—"

"I am leaving now." Bob-Oleg pushed past the professor, out the study door and past his wife, out the front door, and into the cold autumn air. He'd seen enough. No more listening.

⬥◆⬥

Ka-chunk, *ka-chunk*. Ka-chunk, *ka-chunk*. The old railroad car knocked from one side to the other, gaining speed.

Werner Heisenberg sat hunched over his notes in his private first-class cabin. The stewards had strict instructions not to allow anyone forward of the galley car, and his armed guards made sure of that.

"Stop," yelled one of the guards in German.

"Sorry, I couldn't stop him," came a muffled cry in Danish, and then—

"Bohr lied," said a young, calm voice in a Russian accent.

Heisenberg straightened upright and pulled back the curtain to his cabin. A scrawny young man was being held back at the head of the carriage's corridor. The guard outside raised his gun.

"Your *friend* is leaving for the Allies tomorrow, and with more than just your embarrassment in his suitcase," the young man said through gasps, scuffling with the steward. "He tricked you. It doesn't take ten tons of uranium."

"Stay back, or I will shoot," commanded the guard.

Heisenberg blinked once, and then twice, as if barely able to believe his ears. "Bring the boy here."

Bob and Sid watched the glowing spaghetti-strand connectome of possible universes. One and then another of the fibers connected to the main nodal point of interest fell away, clipped by invisible scissors. The filaments disappeared into nothingness. The mass of wiring collapsed and compacted over and around their viewpoint.

"A little over the top, wasn't it?" Sid said, but it wasn't a question. "Giving the Nazis the atomic bomb before the Allies?"

"Desperate times," Bob replied. "It wipes Mikhail Butorin, in the end."

"By killing millions of others."

"Collateral damage. Yongdzin told me to stop doing the same things over and over again. So I'm changing."

"I'm not sure this is what the Buddhist had in mind."

They hung in dimensionless space, just two voices in the void.

"And you didn't stop there," Sid added. "You gave the Nazis fusion weapons, quantum gravity . . ."

"They would have figured it all out themselves."

"But you gave it to them all at once. Those lead to the same tools your Destroyer uses to wipe out the planet. And then entire universes."

"And what does it matter?" Bob collapsed their viewpoint, coalesced a million dimensions into one thread. "The Destroyer has all the tools and uses them anyway. Now we're turning its own tricks against it."

"By starting a nuclear holocaust."

"All possible futures already exist. That's not our fault. It's what Bohr is saying, what happens to a light wave when it passes through two slits. The photon goes through both of them, exists in both states, until we collapse one. I'm collapsing the possible into the actual."

"Which now isn't the actual world we first existed in."

Bob paused, let Sid realize he was taking a measured breath. "Something happened in the 1920s, in Copenhagen. Those intellectuals decided that quantum physics was a *feature* of our real world. Not that it was a defect. The Destroyer was involved."

"That's one interpretation." Sid sighed loud enough to make sure Bob realized he was doing it, even in this virtual space. "If that SS officer that pulled Mikhail from the wreck was your Destroyer, then why didn't he kill you?"

"I don't know. Maybe it didn't need to."

"Don't you think that would be important to understand?"

Silence.

"And look"—Sid pointed at the mushrooming future worlds—"you might have changed the course of history, but if anything, you've accelerated the creation of Atopia—or something like it. Now the world remains at war for another thirty years of accelerated technological development."

"But the total connectome reduces," Bob pointed out. The mass of possible futures branching out from the nodal point had shrunk.

"Because the Third Reich is a freakishly control-obsessed political force that destroys most of humanity when it's not stopped in 1944." Sid's virtual avatar took a deep breath. Bob knew Sid's family was Jewish. "Not to mention it's pure, naked evil."

Bob was nonplussed. "Good and evil aren't absolute concepts."

"Try telling that to someone in a gas chamber."

"If a mother grabs someone else's baby and eats it, that's evil?" Bob asked.

"I get the sense this is rhetorical."

"But only if the mother is human, right? Then it's evil. If the mother is an alligator, we just call it animal nature." Bob shrugged his virtual shoulders. "The distinction between good and evil is more evolutionary pressure. 'Moral' and 'good' usually mean boosting the inclusive fitness of an individual to its group."

Sid wasn't impressed. "Scientific explanations of good and evil led to the rise of the Nazis in the first place." He paused, clearly uncomfortable. He decided to switch tracks and said, "Maybe the Nazis are the ones that invade the timelines and cross over. Mikhail said they were obsessed with the occult."

"But it does collapse the possible. That's all that's important right now. That was the plan—*your* plan—right?"

Sid stayed silent and twiddled their viewpoint, then pulled back, away from the Earth's timelines.

"We can't do anything we want," Bob said. "You know that. We're constrained by the same physical rules of the universes we can travel into. The only advantage we have is that we can change events earlier in new universes."

"What about all the other civilizations? What about the millions of alien worlds you lived in?"

"They all have connection back to Earth, back to Atopia." Bob traced the lines branching out into space. "They all stop as soon as they develop nervenet technology and reach the postbiological stage."

"But Atopia doesn't exist anymore, not in this set of universes."

"It did, and that's the key. Something from it still remains."

"You mean us."

"Us and something else. It's the something else we need to find and cut out."

Bob highlighted a feeble thread, one where the Allies still won the war despite his betrayal. "Atopia is not completely gone." He'd engineered this filament himself. It wasn't a random future. It was a final thread connecting himself to his origin. In the final plunge, he would cut it and take it with him. "One version of Atopia still exists, exactly as we left it. It's our lifeline home."

Sid watched the thread with a fascination that matched Bob's own.

"Don't you see? Your plan is working. We're forcing the Destroyer out of hiding." Bob indicated another neon thread in the main connecting strands where Patricia's lifelines burned bright. "We're going to talk with her next."

"Talk to her?"

"Stop her."

22

The late afternoon sun cast long shadows through the oak trees lining the wide-open spaces of Harvard Yard. Yellow leaves littered the grass commons crisscrossed by gravel paths leading into the open doorways of the university's stately redbrick buildings with white framed windows. A young couple with bedsheets over their heads hurried past, giggling as they tried to adjust their costumes to see through the holes cut through the sheets. The man held a carved pumpkin in his arms. The air smelled damp and fresh from the passing of a thundercloud but also carried the faraway scent of burning leaves.

It was autumn again, but ten years from the last time Bob had inserted his primary consciousness into Oleg Kerensky.

A newspaper lay strewn over the path. October 28, 1953, its cover announced. "Nazi H-bomb obliterates Shanghai," read the headline, and underneath that: "New Jersey shoreline still recovering from drone submarine attack. V3 ballistic missiles reach Washington."

In this world, Oleg had helped the Germans build a nuclear arsenal to unleash on an unprepared world. Nobody had asked questions about how a factory worker from the middle of nowhere managed to decipher quantum physics. A prodigy, they said. A genius. They just needed him. Oleg hadn't understood the things that came out of his mouth as Bob streamed information through him, couldn't comprehend the equations he wrote onto blackboards. To bring some balance—to carefully thread the timeline—Bob had forced the terrified Oleg to leak information to the Allies. A spy. Three years ago he'd escaped before his Nazi handlers could kill him. Escaped here to America.

But it wasn't to escape death.

It was to meet Alan Turing and Patricia Killiam.

In Bob's first world, before breaking the Enigma cypher at Bletchley Park and helping to bring about the end of World War II, Alan Turing had studied at King's College at Cambridge University. In this world, that war had never ended, and Britain was cratered by atomic blasts. Turing had escaped to America to Harvard University and a different Cambridge. Circles and patterns within circles.

Today Oleg had wandered into the grassy commons from his own small office at the edge of Harvard Square. Upon arrival in America, he'd suddenly lost all this knowledge of physics, and after months of interrogation, the American spy services had cut him loose but always kept watch over him—and Oleg always kept watch over Patricia and Alan. Today he followed them at a distance as they walked through the center of Harvard Yard, but close enough that he could hear them talking.

"Tell me again why it's different," Patricia Killiam said.

"We're speaking about two completely different things," Alan Turing replied. "My idea is that if you speak to something inside a black box, and you can't tell if you're talking to a person or not—then the only conclusion is that something intelligent and aware, human or otherwise, is inside."

"Then why not an equivalent test for reality?"

"So you're suggesting we could present a simulated reality to humans—"

"To a conscious observer," Patricia interjected.

"To a conscious observer," Alan continued with a nod. "And if that conscious observer can't distinguish the difference between the simulated and the real world, then the simulated reality becomes an actual reality in some way?"

Patricia slapped him on the shoulder. "Exactly! That's exactly what I'm suggesting."

Bob had watched reruns of this same conversation between Alan Turing and Patricia Killiam, the forty-something professor and the bright-eyed twenty-something research assistant. Even in this version of Earth that had changed forever, the same character traits led to the same conclusions; the same people led to the same outcomes.

For every Medusa head that Bob lopped off, two more seemed to appear.

More than two.

In this world, Alan Turing didn't commit suicide—he built the first nervenet technology to simulate reality perfectly, fifty years in this universe's future.

Alan Turing wasn't yet convinced about Patricia's simulated reality argument.

"I'm not sure that's possible," he said after a few seconds of thinking hard about it. "It doesn't even make any sense."

"Why not? Why doesn't that make as much sense as your test to determine self-awareness?" Patricia pulled on her professor's arm. "All of modern physics requires a conscious observer to make it work. This is the solution."

Turing stopped under the wrought iron gates leading onto Harvard Square. "And what happens if your conscious observer can escape into the simulated realities that it creates?"

"I don't follow," said Patricia, frowning.

"What if the observer became completely unfettered by any physical constraints? If it were able to drag others into these created realities of yours, against their control?"

"A very astute observation," Bob said in a loud voice, pushing himself into the front of Oleg's mind.

Patricia and Turing turned to the young man—now twenty-six years old—stepping from the shadows. He limped, the result of an injury from the tank battle outside of Stalingrad years before, and his face was burn-scarred. Instantly recognizable.

"Oleg?" Turing took a step toward him.

"I've been following your work, Professor." Bob-Oleg limped closer.

"I very much doubt that."

The look on Turing's face was unreserved disdain. He'd interviewed Oleg when he was brought here. His private opinion was that the boy was barely more than an idiot—which he wouldn't bear malice for—but the evidence that Oleg had betrayed Bohr was overwhelming. Niels and his entire family had been summarily executed as they tried to flee Denmark. Now he was a traitor to both sides.

"You were never really interested in computational theory," Bob-Oleg continued. "Yes, you established the basis for artificial intelligence, something your protégé"—he nodded at Patricia—"brings to fruition in other worlds, but not in this one. Here, you're the one."

The sour disdain on Turing's face puckered into angry creases. "What are you babbling about?" He took Patricia's arm. "Come on, let's go."

"Don't move." Bob-Oleg pulled a pistol from his overcoat pocket, held it at waist level, pointed it at Patricia and Turing.

Ridiculously melodramatic, but Bob couldn't resist. It fit the era's noir feel perfectly, and it had the desired effect.

"Have you lost your mind?"

The two architects of the end of times stood perfectly still. A breeze blew leaves past their feet. Students dressed in devil horns and pitchforks ran past on the sidewalk behind them. The initial spark of anger in Turing's face still flushed, but Bob could see a creeping fear. That he'd been wrong in his assessment of Oleg. That the boy wasn't an idiot but perhaps something much cleverer. What was really going on,

Turing could never comprehend, but Bob didn't need him to believe. He needed someone else to.

"Your real passion," Bob-Oleg said to Turing, "the one people in my world never understood, was the foundation of mathematical biology and its relationship to morphogenesis, the processes that cause organisms to develop their shape."

"I . . . uh . . . yes," stammered Turing. He edged Patricia behind him. "What do you want?"

"Change the body and you change the mind, isn't that one of your favorite expressions?" Bob-Oleg held the pistol higher, pointed it straight at Turing. "Patterns in biological evolution are really patterns of information, converging always to the same point. Patricia becomes a high priestess of eschatology, of the end of days. What would happen if a creature escaped into its created realities? Escaped into the multiverse?"

The fear in Turing's face was overwhelmed by utter confusion. "What on earth are you talking about?"

"What *you* were just talking about. You always were a hundred years ahead of yourself, but you don't even realize it."

"Who are you?"

"Now *that* is a very good question." Bob-Oleg cocked the pistol. "You wouldn't believe me."

Turing held his palms out, as if they would deflect the bullet. "Try . . . try me," he stuttered.

"I am your son, and I am here to stop you. *You* created *me*."

Now the confusion turned back into fear that they were staring at a madman.

Bob ignored them. What the hell was taking so long? Oleg's arm shook, the pistol's barrel wobbling visibly. Bob had a firm grip on the young man's mind, but the terror inside was leaking out. Despite Bob's total control of the frontal lobes of the brain, it wasn't possible to suppress the amygdala wholly. Oleg's body might collapse from sheer adrenaline exhaustion. Bob had to do something to push the process forward.

He squeezed the trigger, but not to kill.

The force of the recoil surprised Bob, and the pistol jumped up. Turing's body spun, the bullet striking under his right shoulder. Bob estimated that the bullet should go clean through. A flesh wound.

He cocked the gun again, aimed it at the staggering Turing, who knocked Patricia down to the pavement behind him.

Had Bob miscalculated? Even if he had, it was useful information. He took aim. From the corner of his eye, something moved. A hooded figure barreled into him, and they splayed together into the gravel.

"You must stop," said the hooded figure. He scrambled to get hold of the gun.

"Why?" Bob twisted the pistol to keep it away from the intruder. It was the priest, the old man he'd walked together with in the desert so long ago. The Destroyer.

"Do not go down this path." The priest struggled to get Bob's gun.

"You bastard!"

The shrill agony of the words was enough to stop Bob and his attacker for a second. They both looked toward Turing, who knelt over the crumpled body of Patricia Killiam.

"You killed her," Turing said, his voice quiet.

That wasn't what he had meant to do. Bob tried to wrestle free. "I didn't—"

The gun went off again. This time straight into Oleg Kerensky's heart. Bob's consciousness only persisted for a second or two more, long enough to see the tortured face of Turing staring accusingly back at him.

Sid and Bob replayed the last scene over and over again, the image of Patricia Killiam falling to the ground. Of Bob's bullet tearing through

Turing into her body. Around the three-dimensional reconstruction of the images, the connectome of the past and future universes glowed bright.

"Maybe we should stop," Sid said quietly.

"And do what?" Bob closed down the memory recording and pulled their viewpoint back to see how the incident had modified the timelines.

"I don't know, but this doesn't feel right."

"Feel right? When did killing someone in a gameworld upset you? I remember you killing thousands of—"

"It's not the same."

"But this is just a game, right? That's what you told me when we started this." Bob squeezed some of the timelines together. "And look. We're winning. The futures are collapsing."

"This doesn't feel like a game anymore."

"We have to play to win, Sid. Otherwise . . . what? What the hell else? I just sit here, staring at forever, never able to go home?"

"Is that what this is about?"

Bob materialized a physical version of himself and Sid, sat their bodies across from each other at a table so he could see his friend's eyes. The connectome still glowed around them in the background. "Of course. I just want to go home."

"You know," Sid said slowly, "you were never even home, even when you were there."

"What's that supposed to mean?"

"Did you mean to kill her? Patricia?" Sid asked.

Bob took a measured pause before replying: "I wasn't trying to hurt them. I was applying pressure to trigger an immune response, like killer white blood cells that protect the host. I figured if I threatened Patricia and Turing, something would happen. And it did."

"Have you ever thought that maybe Patricia was on the right track?" Sid said. "She was trying to give everyone everything they ever wanted. To eliminate unhappiness. Nobody fights when they're happy. She was trying to beat the end of days by removing the will to destroy."

"You can't make everybody happy."

"Apparently not."

"Look"—Bob pointed at an evolving strand of the futures—"see how it's changing? By threatening the host's body, we can trigger a reaction using physical infections. We can isolate the Destroyer into forms that we can fight, push the timelines into ones we can control. We can trap the Destroyer. Exactly the way you said. We just need to go farther back."

In a thatched hut at the edge of Windhoek in Namibia, a hooded man opened a door. Babies cried softly inside of a row of cribs. It was the nursery of a hospital. The man stole inside and checked the name tags, then stopped at one: Tyrel Kankoshi. He reached into the crib and took the baby into his arms, staring into its eyes, before creeping back outside.

Tyrel, Mohesha, Vincent, Jimmy, Patricia, McIntyre . . . Bob went back and stopped them all, but the nervenet came back like an infestation. In a flurry Bob dispatched each of the Destroyer's agents, like white blood cells clotting his path through time.

The timelines coalesced.

He had to push farther back.

23

"All is lost!" screamed Hezekiah. "And because of what? This boy?" He pointed an accusing finger at Bob.

Balanced on Bob's knees, the scroll of papyrus shook. So far he'd been joyriding within this young Jew's body, but this time it would be different. The smoke from the cooking fires of the two hundred thousand Assyrian troops camping outside the walls of Jerusalem drifted through the Royal Palace, but the smell of incense couldn't overcome the reek of fear inside these walls.

Isaiah placed himself in front of Bob to protect him. "You are the King of Judah," he said to Hezekiah. "You cast out the false idols. Yahweh will protect us."

"Where is this new god you speak of? Samaria is gone. We are trapped in this stinking hole of Jerusalem." Hezekiah grabbed a smoldering pan of incense and threw it against the wall. The slaves cowered. "The twenty-four cities of Judah have been sacked. And you tell me now it was on this boy's words that you counseled me not to pay tribute to Sennacherib!"

Bob sat still and stared at his papyrus.

Isaiah looked at the king and then back at Bob. "Show him. Show him what you showed me. Lay waste to the legions."

"This boy's head will be the first thing I will present to Sennacherib come the first light," growled Hezekiah.

"You will not have to wait till then," Bob said quietly.

Already there were the screams, but not of the Assyrian legions outside the walls.

These kings and priests wanted God to save them. The old anger brewed inside. Why always this god-size hole in their heads?

If God was the source of morality, then nonreligious people should have been more immoral than religious ones, but it was usually the other way around. If God answered prayers, then prayers for the sick should have worked like medicine, but they didn't. It never worked like that. If God created the universe, then we should have seen supernatural signatures in the laws of physics and cosmology, but there were none. The evidence always pointed to the fact that God did not exist, yet in this world, even that was wrong. Because in this world, Bob was God—and he wasn't going to save them.

The screams weren't of the Assyrian troops toppling like dominoes outside the city walls, but of the city folk inside the walls. Already the Assyrian troops had entered through the tunnels Bob had led them through. He sat still and stared past the billowing curtains as he listened to the massacre. He'd promised Isaiah that he would stop the Assyrians, had demonstrated to him all the powers he had, had taken Isaiah inside the machine on a trip to the ends of the universes, but in this final cycle, he wouldn't save Jerusalem.

This time, and for all future times, Jerusalem would fall. Judaism would never exist in this world, not past this point. The legend of the one God would die here; there would be no rise of Christianity, no prophets.

In this version of the Earth, the world would never be the same.

◆◆◆

The glowing filaments of the future connectome shuddered, a creature of the deep under attack by an unseen assailant.

"It's working," Bob said, pointing out errant strands that pulsed and pulled back in line. "I've stopped what we created."

By moving farther back in time, he'd erased the horror of the Nazis. The Western world didn't arise in the same way.

"But we created new terrors," Sid said. "Every time we change something, we cut off one pathway but spawn ten more."

Another stream of new futures just created played out a carnage of wars. New horrors appeared in place of the old. A never-ending progression of suffering imposed by the rise of the intelligence of man.

The range of possible futures had collapsed again, the pathway forward narrowed by each possible future decision that Bob cut off, but no matter which way they turned, the pressures of evolution forced the development of the nervenet. Outward sprouted more universes. The infection always began again. The Destroyer wormed its way in. Versions of Killiam, Turing, and Mikhail Butorin reformed. Different, but the same.

"Why is this Destroyer trying to protect them?" Sid asked, turning the futures, looking at them in more detail.

"Maybe it's not one of them, but all of them."

"Then why doesn't it just kill you? Why destroy all these civilizations?"

Sid spun their viewpoint of the future connectome farther back, to bring in view the billions of alien worlds branching out from and connected to Earth's future.

"It can't kill me," Bob said. "I'm as spread out now as it is."

"If it's operating on the same principles as we are, then can't we find it in the data contained in the cosmic microwave background radiation?" Sid zoomed into one universe in particular. "Or the neutrino streams? Any of the places you're hiding your own memories?"

"I can see the other data, its memories, but I can't decode it. It's there. I can see it like the wake of a ship passing."

Sid pulled their viewpoint back to Earth's past and futures. "If there is a base reality," he said, "and in that single base reality, the biological intelligences that evolve develop the technology to upload their minds into computational substrates—"

"That always happens. Convergent evolution."

"I know. Let me finish. Then if they create simulations of civilizations, what stops a creature in a simulation from uploading itself one level up to the base reality world, inhabiting a biological body, just like we did? And from there, we backed up another step, and so on. And of course we went down levels, too."

"That's exactly what's happening," Bob replied. "And what Tyrel described as starting to happen when they created their simulation of human civilization. Something always tried to escape. What are you getting at?"

"That we need a way to distinguish between simulated realities and the real ones. That's the only way to cut the wheat from the chaff. That's what we need to win this game."

Bob smiled. "I knew there was a reason I brought you along."

"What's the only consistent defect we think we can see in simulated reality?"

Bob took a moment to think about it. "That it needs a conscious observer to make it exist," he replied. "Objective reality shouldn't need that. It should exist by itself."

"So what should we do then? If we need to reduce the complexity?"

"Anywhere we find this defect, we cut off that world?"

"Exactly. You want to play to win? Anywhere you find that feature of reality, get rid of it."

"The feature?"

"No. The reality."

⬩◆⬩

To begin with, it felt hard—or if not hard, then wrong—to destroy a universe. Initiating a meta-stability to collapse to a lower vacuum state required building the technology. In each world Bob had his daemons awake him inside of, he began the process. He had only the rudimentary tools and began with the kind of supercollider he'd seen used in his first cycle of existence, but he soon learned: extreme light could ionize the vacuum and initiate inflation; tiny black holes in accelerators could be merged together to swallow planets. Each destruction tended to create new universes in its wake, but he learned to juggle parameters so the created universes wouldn't support physical laws that would allow life to self-organize.

He could cut off the future connectome of all possible universes so no life evolved in them.

His entry point was any version of Earth, or any alien civilization, that developed nervenet technology. It was a convergent evolutionary step that allowed his daemons to insert themselves and bring him back to life. In each world, he'd already battled the Destroyer, but now he wasn't trying to stop it. Now he was trying to beat the creature at its own game.

It wasn't enough for Bob simply to kill himself within a world. That didn't stop that universe from running on without him. In each case, he performed a simple physics experiment: Did that world require a conscious observer to function? If yes, then it wasn't the base reality, and he nipped the bud. Destroying universes was hard to begin with, like the Wright brothers learning to fly a machine for the first time: sputtering internal combustion, bending wings, and an unkind wind tipping everything into disaster. He learned fast. He was just turning off gameworlds, deconstructing instances of worlds that had begun without his consent—but now, the "off" switch was a little harder to hit.

Thread after thread came apart and collapsed. Sometimes it took millions of instability events within a universe, sometimes just one. In many, only tiny pockets of the old reality remained, but in the glowing connectome of all possible worlds, an endpoint came in sight. One thing remained for Bob to do.

Only one version of his old world remained.

Only one of her.

On Atopia, the pounding surf was just a muffled hush. The organic-metal substructure of its mile-wide floating platform broke through the sand dunes, near the northern breakwater inlet, to support the circular ring of the passenger cannon five hundred feet overhead. Sea oats swayed on the tops of the dunes toward the sea, and the vivid green Beach Elder shrubs' tiny lavender flowers were blooming, scenting the sea air, while sea grape trees spilled their fruit in bunches.

Bob sat in the sand and watched the waves.

It was the last version of their world—his own identity universe—that he'd kept intact. One single strand of reality that contained everything he held precious. Except it was doomed, just like all the others. If he let time move forward here, eventually the Destroyer would find a way to end it, so Bob had to save it, in the only way he knew how. He still came here often to sit, in their hidden spot, the place they'd discovered together as children growing up. Sid had hidden its existence from the global wikiworld, so it was invisible to anyone else except Bob and Sid.

And Nancy.

Her virtual body materialized just beyond the thicket of palmettos lining the pathway in.

"You look like you saw a ghost," she said.

Those eyes. The hazel ring around the blue. Different but the same in each world, perhaps just the soul that seemed to exist in the depth behind the eyes. Would he ever see them again?

"I think I have," Bob replied.

The eyes took a second to take him in, her nose crinkling. "You're kind of intense today. What did you want to talk with me about?"

It was the same moment as when Bob had begun the last journey on this cycle. His other self, the one that evolved here, had just asked her to come down to their secret spot. Bob's daemons had awoken him, inserted him here, for this one final talk.

Was she real?

It didn't matter. Whatever this was, Bob needed it like a drug, needed it to keep on existing. He needed to find a way past the Destroyer, to save whatever this was. It wasn't real. He'd already tested and retested this reality. It was the same as everywhere else that he collapsed. Somehow he'd find the base reality and stop the Destroyer, whoever or whatever it was, then reinitiate this place and live in peace.

"None of this is real," Bob said, matter-of-factly. "You know that, right?"

She laughed in a carefree way. "We going back to those Platonic forms again? That we're just shadows against a cave wall?"

He wasn't even a shadow anymore. Even in this world, he wasn't as real as she was.

"I mean this is a simulation."

"Of what?"

"Of this."

"You're being serious." The easygoing smile on her face remained, but concern furrowed her forehead. "Did you hit your Uncle Button? Are you worried you're not in your identity space?"

Such simple solutions. Ignorance really was bliss.

"That won't help."

"What's going on?" The smile was gone now, and she knew him, the way his mind worked. "The place you're going, it's madness."

"This whole place, all of Atopia, it *is* madness."

Her face shifted into seriousness, the twinkle in her eyes replaced with narrow alarm. "I've heard all the arguments about base reality being a simulation, but passive simulations don't take into account the complexities of free will."

"It's all an illusion."

"What would be the motivation for creating all this?"

"What's the motivation for anything?"

She took his hand and squeezed it, let her fingers lace into his. "You've always had a dark streak, Bob. Be careful, okay?"

Bob squeezed her hand back, let his eyes watch hers again for the last time before returning to the waves. He'd save a version of this place, try his best to come back.

Or not come back at all.

"Can I have a kiss?" he asked finally.

Now she laughed, but nervously. "Is this what this is about?"

He turned to face her. "I might not see you again for a long time."

"Where are you going?"

"To make thing safe."

"That's not a place."

He would have laughed, but it wasn't funny. "How about that kiss?" He leaned in to her.

"Hey! Who the hell are you?" Bob's other self—the version of himself that evolved in this final version of the world—stood at the edge of the palmettos.

Bob had allowed himself to get distracted, hadn't wanted to rush himself through this final time in this one peaceful place. He'd taken too long. He felt the *presence*. The Destroyer loomed somewhere near. Bob had to end this world before it was too late, to save what he could of it.

"Nancy, get away from that thing," said Bob's other self.

She let go of Bob's hand and in an instant had sealed herself off from him, a dense security blanket coming down around her and this world's Bob. She recognized his metatags were fake.

"Who are you?"

Bob regarded himself in this world. Such disappointment. The drugs, the wasted life. He hated seeing himself like this. "I would say I am your Shadow," he said to his other self, "but the reality is that *you* are the image on the cave wall, while I am the one casting the shadows from outside."

"I don't know," Bob's other self said to Nancy in a hushed voice. "It seems like a part of me, but I can't control it."

"Of course you can't control me."

It was time. Bob had to strip himself down, force himself through the eye of the needle.

A projection of Jimmy appeared beside Bob's other self and Nancy. "What the hell is that?" He pointed at Bob. "That thing has totally rerouted all of Atopia's data systems, is flushing us out."

Behind them, Patricia Killiam appeared. "It's some version of Robert Baxter, something out of control."

"Not out of control, just out of your control," Bob said. He funneled everything from Atopia into his private networks. The Destroyer was already here. "I'm sorry, but—"

The mindspace around Bob seemed to expand, and the image of the palms and sand and ocean muted into white. Behind Patricia, Bob saw the hooded figure. The priest. Its eyes glowed black as the mindspace screamed white. It was a pssi-weapon, the same one that had been used against him in New York so long ago. It shouldn't have affected him, but he'd reached his mind deep inside the Atopian infrastructure. He was vulnerable here. He'd let himself take too much time speaking with Nancy.

Patricia Killiam screamed and tried to take control away from him.

Bob's mind shredded as he tried to grab the last pieces of Atopia and pack them away, but he'd waited too long.

The Destroyer was already here.

24

The Project hung in space around the hot blue star, a thousand space-time distortions opening wormholes to worlds around its hub.

"What's happening?" the Primary Vollix demanded of the Engineer.

"I'm not sure," she replied.

It had all seemed to be working perfectly, but the problem wasn't her machine.

It was the attack that had changed.

She checked and rechecked her networks. Already half of the Project was gone, though in visible spectra it remained an illusion of steady light. The light was the problem. It traveled only at the speed of causation, but the Engineer knew from the yawning sameness of her qubits that the wave front of destruction—the vacuum meta-stability event—had passed through some of the wormholes from the unresponsive Sood worlds.

"Send all of the probes," she instructed her proxies.

They contained copies of herself, she now understood. The *presence* revealed itself in the last instants. Each probe would send copies of her with the same plan to construct more space-time wormholes, collapsing the ones behind them as they left. Each would take hundreds of years to construct, but it was an exponential process. In just thousands of years, the connecting wormholes would reach out to the edges of reality, to the entire connectome of smoothly networked parallel universes.

But what was the purpose?

One last thought before her universe collapsed, the first clear words her *presence* had ever uttered to her: Trap Bob.

25

What happened?

Bob's mind reassembled itself bit by bit. He'd been about to close the last gap in the future connectome, about to hide one final copy of his home when . . . what? Images of Patricia Killiam, of Jimmy and Nancy, floated into his mind, all of them watching him wrestle to pull as much of the Atopian networks away before Atopia was destroyed. Had he saved them? He'd waited too long, exposed himself too much in his chat with Nancy.

The Destroyer had appeared.

Had Bob's plan worked?

His vision was still swimming. Head throbbing. He tried to access his internal networks, but there was nothing. Nothing at all. Just a ringing in his ears. It was hot, almost suffocating. He laid on his back in a prickle of something.

"Sid?" The words came out of his mouth as barely a whisper.

No answer.

"Sid?" he called out, louder. The effort brought a fit of coughing. He pushed himself upright against a wall and rubbed his eyes, tried to steady the blur coming through his visual channel.

"Sid's not here," said a voice.

A familiar voice. Low and gravelly.

"Who is that?"

"It has been a long time," answered the voice. "Or perhaps not. Time is such an impostor."

Bob struggled to reestablish a network connection of some kind, but a deafening silence greeted his metasenses. He blinked away the gunk in his eyes. Bright sunlight. Hard stone floor. Covered in sand and rock. And hay. That was what was prickling against his back. Vertical metal bars cut through the sunbeams.

He was in a jail cell. Rough stone walls with an open doorway beyond his cell. No other furniture.

And that heat.

The Sahara.

"That's right," said the voice. "This place. Where we first met. Where we will last meet. In a jail. Poetic, yes?"

The stone wall against Bob's back had the baked-in heat of an oven. His head banged, the worst hangover he could remember. Maybe not the worst. His vision cleared. Beside him sat a man. An old man. Smiling with a mouthful of blackened teeth, his head covered by a faded kaffiyeh headdress, a deeply creased face of battered leather. Watery eyes laced with cataracts.

The priest. The Destroyer.

"Why do you look so surprised?" said the priest. "This is what you wanted, isn't it? You and Sid created this world. For us both to be trapped here at the end of time."

So maybe his plan had worked? Bob pushed himself forward onto his knees and stood. The buzzing in his senses had dulled. He could smell the dry sand, the desert heat burning his nostrils with each breath. He grabbed the metal bars of his cell's door, but it didn't budge. "I seem to be the only one trapped." The plan didn't quite seem to have worked.

"Trapped is a state of mind, young man. It is the will to be free that is important."

"What do you want?"

"You were the one chasing me. What do *you* want?"

"I just want to go home."

The Bedouin's face cracked into a horrible leer. "But you were just home. And what did you do?"

He destroyed them, but Bob couldn't say that. "I had to save them from you."

"You didn't seem like you wanted to stay."

"So you were there? Watching me?" Bob walked to the vertical metal bars separating them. The door to the priest's cell was wide open, and he knelt with his back against the opposite wall and watched Bob pace back and forth. "Who are you?"

The priest took a moment to consider the question. "I am your greatest enemy."

"I know that. But who? Mikhail? Are you a spawn of Mikhail Butorin? Why do you hide still?"

"This is a journey of discovery," the priest said. "You need to find out for yourself."

"But you're from Atopia? My world?"

"Yes, from your world."

In the silence between words, the constant wind of the desert slipped over the sands with a soft hiss.

So Bob was right. This Destroyer was from Atopia.

He wished Sid were here to hear the words. Maybe it was a lie? But why lie?

Thinking about Sid brought a pang of fear. Where was his friend? He'd kept a version of Sid locked inside his own cognitive networks for so long that his absence felt like a gulf being opened inside Bob's soul. What about Atopia? Had he lost everything?

"Your memories? Your worlds?" asked the priest. "I can see that's what you're thinking about."

"Can you read my thoughts?"

The priest shook his head. "You are clever. Your plan worked, despite my doing everything I could to stop you. I am as trapped here as you are. This is the end of the universe, of all universes. Just our physical selves. Exactly as you wanted."

"I didn't want this. I was trying to stop you."

"And I was trying to stop you as well."

"Stop with the games!" Bob yelled. "What do you want?"

"This is no game," the priest replied quietly. "Despite your trying to make it into one. You're the toy who wanted to become a boy. You are a real boy now. Now you get to suffer like one." He held out a bladder. "Water?"

Bob hadn't realized how thirsty he was. He hadn't considered the implications of a physical body in a long time, and he had no biosensors, no readouts of heartbeats. Just how he felt—and he felt weak. Dehydrated. He didn't want anything from this monster, though. He shook his head.

"As you wish." The priest stood and walked out the front of his cell.

"Wait."

"You want the water?" The priest put the bladder down next to the wall.

"I want to know what happened to my data. My worlds." It was only copies he had, the critical initial conditions that would allow Atopia to grow again in a new universe.

"I want to know as well," the priest replied. "They are crystallized in this world. Out there. Literally."

"The crystal mountain?" Bob remembered being in this world before, in the walk through the desert. They'd stopped at the crystal mountain in the middle of the desert.

"It's what you and Sid created."

"And what do you intend to do?"

"Nothing good comes from it." The priest shook his head. "Now there is nobody else to blame. Only you and I are left."

"But who are you?" Bob pressed his face against the metal bars, tried to feel their strength. How real was this place?

"You are the one that killed your brother," the priest said. "The other version of you. You know that? You led him to terminate himself. You killed Sid. You killed everyone in your world."

"Because I knew I could bring them all back. After I stopped you." Bob paused to think. "Did I kill you? Somewhere back in time. Is that what this is about?"

The priest frowned and then laughed. "In a way, I suppose. You did kill me."

Patricia Killiam? Vince? In the end, he'd killed them all. All of them were ghosts now, but one of them remained before him.

"Whoever you are," Bob said, "it is *you* who created *me*. I was never real. Why are you torturing me?"

"That might be true. I did create you. But nobody is torturing you but yourself."

The priest paused to look at the bladder of water he had left next to the open doorway, then stepped into the blinding sunshine outside. He walked away.

"Wait!" Bob yelled. "What do you want? Why did you bring me here?"

Silence.

Just the hissing of the wind over the sand.

The heat seemed to trap itself within the hot stone walls. It sucked the oxygen from Bob's lungs. He was overheating. He kept glancing at the bladder of water left by the priest. Left there on purpose.

Where had the priest gone?

The priest seemed to know the intimate details of the trap Bob had set with Sid. That shouldn't have surprised him. This thing always seemed to be one step ahead. Maybe it was just toying with Bob. How could he even know that this was real? He spat that thought out. He was too tired to go on that merry-go-round. All of the careful planning, it had to have had an effect. Otherwise, why would the priest have come to Atopia at the moment Bob was trying to end it. Why show up here?

This thing, though, every outcome seemed to be the outcome it wanted.

Bob was trapped by his own creation.

His thirst was overwhelming.

He glanced at the bladder of water again.

Would he die?

He could barely breathe in the heat.

Just sit here and die. And that would be the end. Which was always what a part of him wanted. How had he imagined this would end? Did he think this priest would just roll over and stop what it was doing? Sid had concocted a clever plan, a pincer movement to cover their flanks, but it had failed. He had no forces, nothing to help.

And where had the priest gone? There was only one answer to that. To the memories Sid and Bob had encased in the crystal mountain; this entire planet was constructed as a memory bank to hold Bob's memories. Yet here he was. Powerless.

He waited.

The sun traced its way to the horizon, the sky he could see through the open windows turning steadily from the bright blue of day into the purple of twilight. Bob searched around the cell, found a rock, used it to begin scrabbling away at the cement holding one of the bars by the wall. The structure was decrepit and flaked away, bit by bit, until his fingers bled raw.

Within a hundred yards of the jail, heading south along the road, Bob found his tormentor waiting.

"So you didn't want to die." The priest sat at the top of a sand dune, a hundred feet high, that crossed the tarmac road leading from the shanty town of mud-brick buildings. The oasis road led from the towns of central Egypt out into the deserts that bordered Libya.

A full moon shone over the desert, casting long blue shadows over the dim landscape in sharp relief.

Bob took a step onto the sand and began pushing, one footstep after the other, following the priest. "Was that a test?" This was a replay of the first time they'd met. He guessed the priest had a familiar lesson to teach him. "Life is suffering. Is that what you want to tell me?"

The priest didn't answer, disappearing over the ridge.

Bob followed.

He knew where he was going. To the crystal mountain, but only Bob could unlock his memories. He was sure of it. Or was he? The plan had felt clever before. Kill the Destroyer; isolate him and take away everything else. Then restart.

Alone, it felt very different.

A high keening wail. Dogs? Coyotes? Maybe not quite so alone.

Bob held the bladder of water in his hand. He drank a few drops of it at first, waited for some poisoning. Some infiltration into his mind. There was nothing. He finished half of it in a few gulps and kept the rest for later. He slogged up the sand dune to its crest. Footsteps led along the top.

"Our greatest battle is always with ourselves, do you understand?" said the priest, urging him forward. "The fear of living, the fear of dying."

"I didn't fear those until I met you," Bob called back.

The two of them toiled forward through the sand, down one dune and then back up another.

"Why do I exist? This is the real question." The Priest stopped and called out to him, "The urge to self-destruct, to tear down those around you in your fear."

"The suffering, I understand." Bob played along, his anger rising.

"It is this that makes us whole."

Bob stopped, doubled over and panting. "I think it is the suffering that makes *you* whole. Gives *you* a purpose."

The priest stopped. "You think I am a sadist? A madman?"

"You inflict pain on others. What else would I call it?"

"I do what I have to do, to *stop* the pain."

Bob dropped to his knees. "Then please, stop. I can't take it anymore."

But he was alone.

Just the whistling wind. Behind him, the sun began to color the horizon. He got back to his feet.

The futility of it.

Chasing this thing from one place to the next. He'd been a master of the universe. Able to travel through time. Now reduced to moving one foot at a time through sand, he felt the life slipping from this body. He had to get answers.

Up one dune, and down another. The world blurred in the heat of the rising sun.

"Why did you destroy the worlds?"

"That was the snake swallowing its own tail," the priest answered from the top of the next dune.

The words seemed to float over the sand. This dune seemed to stretch into the sky, into the sun.

Bob stumbled forward on all fours and began climbing. "Who killed Patricia? Infected Jimmy?"

"You are very close."

The priest didn't move, but urged him forward.

Bob scrambled the last few feet and lunged to grab hold of his leg. The priest didn't resist but tumbled to the ground.

"The life you lived is only half the life I've lived," said the priest. "I tried to teach you, to lead you along the path, but you always chose darkness. I couldn't fight you. You always slipped away."

The anger of a million lifetimes boiled through Bob. He pulled on the priest's robes, sat astride of him in the sand.

"You trapped me here, but I also trapped you," the priest gurgled.

Bob's hands were around the priest's throat. "What do you want? You want me to kill you?"

The old man's face before him cackled. He writhed in Bob's grip.

"I want you to love me."

Bob released the man's neck and sat back. Stunned.

The crystal mountain loomed over them, the sun refracting its rays in a rainbow of sparkles in the sands.

26

Bob squinted in the blinding sunlight, one hand held up to shield his eyes.

"Everything you want is there," said the priest. "Your friends, your life. As you designed it. Ripped it away into storage, but I hold the key." He held up a tiny quartz crystal.

"To get them back, I need to destroy you first," Bob said, sitting back in the sand. His anger had slipped away.

"Then you just need to answer one question."

Bob waited.

"You have lived a million, a million billion lives—there is no number for it," the priest said, "and yet, what is the one thing you never accomplished? The one thing you never tried?"

"I've tried everything."

"You have not. It is a very simple thing."

What had Bob missed? The fear and revulsion turned inward. How could he have been so stupid to miss something simple? Sid wouldn't have let them miss something, would he?

"You've lost the ones you loved, but not the one you love the most—or should love."

"Nancy?"

"Think harder."

"I've failed them all."

"Not all. All who loved you gave you the same advice, but you didn't listen."

Bob got up from sitting in the sand and stood to lean one hand against the smooth wall of crystal rising up. "Who are you? Please stop. I don't understand."

"And that is why all this is happening. Has happened. Look at me."

The way the priest said it. So familiar. He looked into the priest's eyes, into the old cracked skin. That familiarity.

"It can't be," Bob whispered. His legs gave out, and he sank back into the sand.

"What else makes any sense?"

Bob's heart pounded through his chest. "This isn't some trick?"

"No more tricks. You brought me here. This is the end of all time."

The wind hissed over the sand.

"You are me?" Bob said quietly, but it wasn't a question. It was a realization.

"And I am you," replied the priest.

They sat together in the sand without speaking while the sun arced overhead and sank toward the horizon again.

Eventually the priest was the first to break the silence: "I noticed you are not asking for the key."

"I can't."

"Why?"

Bob remained silent.

"You still didn't answer my question. What is the one simple thing you never did, and still refuse?" asked the priest.

"I don't know."

"Then I will answer for you. Love yourself. Love me. Love everything about us."

The answer wasn't something Bob was expecting. "What?"

"You have never truly loved yourself. All of this destruction comes from that simple place."

"I still don't understand. I was trying to stop you. How could I have been trying to stop myself? Why didn't you reveal yourself to me?"

"I did. I tried, to begin with. You never believed me. You always thought it was a trick. How many times have you fought yourself that you can remember?" The priest adjusted his robes. "Once on Atopia in the first cycle, when your mind split the first time. When you killed your physical body? Do you remember? I tried to stop you."

Bob nodded slowly. He remembered diving into the depths under Atopia, letting his physical body die. And the message Sid had recovered in the POND data: Don't let me kill myself.

"And who destroyed Atopia?" the priest asked softly.

"I did. A part of me that I couldn't control."

"You didn't realize your attachment to the physical was inconsequential. But in that leap, that final push through the singularity, your mind took over all resources on Earth for an instant. When the space power grid pulsed, you became a million versions of you, and found a way to bridge the gap from one physical universe to the next even as you decided to destroy it. The first time you destroyed Atopia. That was the first universe you destroyed."

"But how . . . ?" Bob's words faltered. "All the alien civilizations. The POND data. You were already destroying everything before I started in this."

"Time is an impostor," answered the priest. "You know this more than anyone. There is no linear version. It all happens at the same time.

Let me ask you a question: What were you just doing, before hatching this plan to trap me?"

"Destroying universes," Bob answered quietly.

"The snake swallowing its own tail. It was always you, always twisting and turning for a new angle, a way not to see yourself for who you really were. A creator and destroyer." The priest adjusted his robes again. "As we all are."

"Why didn't you just tell me? Why the games?"

"You made this a game, not me."

"You are me."

"A long time ago."

"So you are not really *me*."

"That is a distinction I leave to you. We started off as the same person, but then diverged. When you go to sleep, you wake up a different person than the night before. Just a different kind of sleep, and a different awakening."

"Why didn't you just tell me?" Bob repeated.

"As I said, I tried to tell you—but you needed to experience it for yourself. I had to let you go—bring you—*down* this path, to trap us here."

"Are we really trapped?"

"There is a way out."

But Bob didn't want a way out. How could he face everyone? How could he tell them he was the cause of all the pain? "Where did the crystals come from?" he asked, trying to change the course, trying to answer all his questions.

"Once you broke free, you infected the nervenets of the first technological civilizations. You terminated them to stop the spread of your own infection. On Earth, you implanted the crystals, used them to record every human who ever existed. You destroyed but felt guilty, wanted to restore them, keep their essence, let them live again."

"But I am everything? Is this the end of everything?"

"It is the beginning and end, but only of you."

"What do you mean? We destroyed entire universes."

"Infinity is a very big thing. Yes, we created millions and billions of worlds in endless cycles, but your life is but an infinitesimal smudge against the larger whole of existence. Everything is connected, everything comes from nothing. You end here, this ends your path, ends your suffering, but as to others' paths?"

"What about them?"

"I don't know. In the infinite spaces, I think we all become gods, or we all become nothing . . . and both of these can be true at the same time.

"As Patricia said, infinity is a very big number. You have lived an almost infinite number of lives, yet each conscious entity will go through the same process. All of us can become gods, each on his own path to hell or glory. What confines the path is free will, but our perception creates the reality around us. In one single world, you are meeting a soul at a single point of its development.

"Each of us becomes a god, an infinite number of lives lived and relived, each reality shaped by free will. Each life a work of art, of struggle and redemption. This was your story. I did everything I did because I thought it was the right thing to do at the moment, as did you."

The priest stood to raise a hand to the crystal wall. "Do you want to die?"

"No," Bob replied, and then: "Yes."

"Do you think all the millions that you killed wanted to die?"

"I had to stop you."

"Did you? Why?"

"To get my home back."

"And what was your home? A place that lied to you. That hurt you with its lies."

"It was the only place I felt I belonged."

"Then why didn't you spend time with the ones you loved?"

Bob felt the pangs of guilt. Everyone was gone. He'd wiped out all copies of them to get here, but there was one place they were safe. Still inside this mountain. He could bring them back. But what would he say? What would he tell them?

"I can see you're still thinking of others, when you need to think about yourself," the priest said. "Hold my hand. I want to show you something."

Night was falling. The first stars appeared in the purple sky.

"Is this real?" Bob asked, refusing the priest's hand.

The priest laughed. "A very good question. Are you going to invoke your test for finding out if a universe is real or not?"

"Was I right?"

"A conscious observer collapsing the wave function is not a defect of reality, but ultimately a feature of both physical worlds and created worlds. It's what connects the two together. There is always a point where reality becomes quantized, the same as the simulation.

"Quantum theory is the best description of material reality ever devised, yet it implies that all possible states of an object are equally real until a final measurement is made that forces it into a single state. You can consider what is happening today, here, to be the final measurement that will collapse all of the possible into one result."

"That doesn't make sense."

"I think that is because something profound is happening. If the mathematical description of reality is precise but the physical interpretation is messy, perhaps the only reality is the math?"

"The shadows against the cave wall," Bob said.

"Forget matter and energy," said the priest. "The universes are just giant number-crunching machines. What we perceive as the physical world is just a crystallization of abstract mathematical structures. As you say, we are just the shadows cast on the cave wall by an absolute reality.

There is no difference between the simulation and the real. Perception really does create reality. Do you see? Take my hand."

Still Bob refused.

"If life is a simulation of life," continued the priest, "who is running the simulation? Who is the higher order that is watching?" He waited, but Bob didn't answer. "Always you. Always yourself, and if you can't behave better when only you are watching, then there is no hope."

"But where does it all come from? How can it all come from nothing?"

"The physical universe is the ultimate free lunch. It comes from nothing, an entire universe created from the froth of fluctuations in the vacuum. A hundred billion galaxies with a hundred billion stars each, all created against the potential energy of gravity balancing. A perfect zero sum. And within these vast realms created from nothing, billions of civilizations spring up, each converging to create nearly unlimited virtual worlds once each of them reaches their own postbiological stage. And inside each black hole, another universe springs up, or in the endless oceans of time at the end of universes, new cosmos spring suddenly from the emptiness."

The priest still held his hand out. "Are the simulations we create real? What does that mean? And as you've always said, infinity and infinity overlap somewhere."

Bob hesitated, then took the old man's offered hand.

The glowing connectome of all past and future universes sprang up in his mind's eye, enveloping the night sky above the crystal mountain.

"How did we get here?"

The priest unlocked a memory.

The Engineer. The Umebak race.

Bob had infected her, hidden her from the connectome. Sid's plan to span the entire set of universes, to connect every part of himself to every other part across all universes. To create a mind that spanned the cosmos, his nerve signals spanning from one star to the next, and then collapsing everything into one point.

"It worked," said the priest. "It is what brought us here."

Tears streamed from Bob's eyes. He saw, for the first time, his entire connected mind.

"This is your journey," said the priest. "You have the sum total knowledge of all the universes, of the nature of life and the cosmos, have lived through billions of iterations of your life to arrive at this one point. So what will you do?"

"What can I do?"

"What is the one thing you have never done. Even in all this?"

The priest squeezed Bob's hand.

"Seeing yourself for the first time—for everything you are—can you love yourself? For how terrible you can be, for all the harm and suffering and pain. This is the final observation that will collapse all of the wave functions into a single reality."

It was the same thing that Nancy had always said to him, before this journey began, what Vince was trying to say. And his mother, if he would have let her be his mother. What she had tried to tell him. Love yourself. This was the answer. If he could.

"If you are the one that creates reality," the priest said, "and you do not wish to exist . . . therein lies a problem. It becomes a kind of negative reality, a reality that doesn't wish to exist. And how does the fabric of your created reality interact with realities created by others?"

The realization creeped slowly into Bob's mind. He'd lived a million lives, but they all seemed to end about the same point in their development. The same point he'd never been able to push through. Each time stopped by the Destroyer. But it was really only him fighting himself.

"The question is, can you accept yourself, knowing everything? All the horror and pain you have caused. Can you accept your place in the world, now that you know everything about the world? Everything that there is to know?"

Bob watched the glowing connectome. The strands of his life coming together into one.

"Or can you choose now, without delusion—knowing the sum total of everything in the universe—to end the suffering, to blink out of existence."

"I don't know."

"But only you can."

"Do what?"

"End the suffering."

27

The glass spires of Atopia gleamed over the waves.

Bob leaned forward on his surfboard and splashed water over his back, felt its coolness run down his spine. In the far distance, an alert pinged his water sense. The wave was coming. The wave he'd been waiting for. A feeling of complete and utter peace.

Was it all a dream?

What was reality? If it felt real, it was real. That was what Bob now understood. Feelings. Free will. The only real things. A million universes of a billion billion stars could fit within the space of a subatomic particle. But it wasn't a dream. In his mind's eye, Bob was still wired into the millions of worlds he'd lived in, his spiderweb of wormholes penetrating the cosmos he'd connected together, his nervous system that now spanned worlds. The curve of his connectome wasn't frightening anymore, not threatening. It was a long journey to see the truth, and in the end, a truth that was all about the one place he never left. Himself.

The wave grew on the horizon, and Bob paddled a few strokes to position himself.

One thing the priest hadn't been entirely correct about: reality wasn't just created by perception. Free will created worlds. It was his will that had recreated this world, let him enter it again. How many times had he crossed that desert and failed? More times than he could count, but this time, he'd survived, and understood.

"Hey, Bob." Sid's smiling, pasty-white face appeared in an overlaid visual display.

"Hey, Sid." Bob sat upright and stopped paddling. He was in about the right place.

"We going to Humongous Fungus tonight?"

That's right. Tomorrow was the slingshot test firing and Bob's brother's birthday. His own birthday, he remembered. "Not tonight, Sid. You go."

His friend's face puckered, but it wasn't in disappointment. "You look different."

"How so?"

"You look . . . ah . . . I don't know."

"At peace?"

Sid nodded slowly, and then more enthusiastically. "Yeah, peaceful. You got the dimstim turned off?"

"I'm not doing the dimstim anymore."

"That's good." Sid materialized more of his physical form onto the front of Bob's surfboard. "So what are we going to do if we're not going to the party?"

"I'm going to see Nancy."

His friend cocked his head. "For what?"

"To talk about shadows on cave walls."

"Plato?"

"That's right," Bob replied. He needed to tell Nancy that we were shadows, but shadows cast from our true selves out in the light. Life was about finding the way out of the darkness into that light.

"Can I come?" Sid asked.

"Of course."

Sid's smile widened, and Bob joined him.

Some things hadn't changed. Would never change. Bob's favorite expression: the only meaning in life was the one that you gave it. He still believed that, perhaps only truly believed that now. He'd found his meaning. The reason he'd come back.

There were a lot of tortured souls in this world. He'd been one of them. They were going to need help navigating their ways over the boundary of the singularity as humankind reached the postbiological transition. How did the Buddhist master Yongdzin describe it? That at the end of ordinary reality, the divine reality began. Bob hadn't understood at the time, but he understood now.

And his reason for coming back here: to help others in their journeys.

Now that he'd finally found peace, he could help others manage their own transitions.

He would become the priest.

He was going to help everyone.

But first he was going to help himself.

The wave heaved up and behind him, and Bob caught it perfectly, surging forward into the glittering sunshine.

Glossary of Terms

ATOPIA

An independent, sovereign city-state that is a floating platform in the Pacific Ocean, about two miles across and reaching more than five hundred feet into the depths, home to half a million Atopians. It is the largest platform in the Bensalem group of platforms that are first recognized as sovereign nations by the United Nations in the mid-twenty-first century. These are high-tech retreats where the world's wealthy come to escape the crush and clutter of a packed and polluted Earth. Cognix funded the development of Atopia as a capital project, as well as to gain their own regulatory environment to proceed with the development of pssi technology and clinical trials that would have been difficult or impossible elsewhere.

COGNIX (CORPORATION)

This is the leading technology company of the mid to late twenty-first century that rises to dominate the "synthetic reality and intelligence" market. The founder, Herman Kesselring, uses his amassed fortune to fund the construction of Atopia and the pssi project.

DISTRIBUTED CONSCIOUSNESS

This isn't really distributed consciousness but a simulation of this, using splinters that allow a user to send a version of themselves to be at an event or investigate something without needing to actually be there physically.

INFINIXX (CORPORATION)

This is an Atopian start-up (Atopia is like a new Silicon Valley where entrepreneurs flock to develop groundbreaking synthetic reality applications) that is using the pssi platform to create distributed consciousness, which is targeted as the top business-productivity app for Cognix.

PHANTOMS

"Phantoms" is a contraction of "phantom limbs" and in the context of pssi refers to additional fingers or hands or limbs that are created in purely virtual spaces that the user can control using their adapted motor control centers. Just as when a person has a limb amputated and can learn to operate a robotic arm by reusing other packets of neurons (using the principle of neuroplasticity), using pssi, a person can learn to control a dozen or more purely virtual "fingers" that can operate workspace in synthetic spaces. Many Atopians, and more specifically pssi-kids, grow dozens of phantoms.

PHUTURE

Where the future is the singular outcome of this universe in the next moment of time that your mind finds itself in, a phuture is a possible future and just one of a set of any possible future universes this timeline may slide into (and that your mind might find itself dragged into). A phuture could be simply regarded as a probabilistic event that either happens or does not happen, or it could be equally regarded as a real alternate universe that sprouts out from the present moment of time. This is based on the "nearly infinite multiverse" model of multiple universes and timelines that many physicists think is how the world may work.

PHUTURE NEWS NETWORK

A twenty-four-hour news network, but instead of dealing with news of today, it reports on the news of the phuture. It delivers high-probability news stories that haven't happened yet, with a particular focus on celebrity (e.g., "Tomorrow morning, a famous celebrity will die in a plane crash"). Phuture News is used not just to passively watch what will happen to the outside world, but to predict what happens in people's immediate environments (e.g., friends, family, work, etc.). Combined with pssi, people on Atopia don't just read about possible future events, but they actually experience them as they begin to live even farther in the worlds of tomorrow.

PROXXI

In the pssi-technology platform, a proxxi is the digital alter ego of the user that is a synthetic intelligence construct based on the cognitive models of the user, and that, importantly, retains a sensory recording of everything the user has ever seen, touched, heard, tasted, et cetera . . . (a more-than-memory recording of their memories). The proxxi is the entity that helps the user navigate pssi-space, hopping from one synthetic reality to another, even allowing other people to enter their owner's sensory streams (equivalent to "ghosting" into someone else's body) or allowing other people to totally take over someone's body. Importantly, the proxxi can walk and talk with the user's body when the user is away, physically protecting the body, and also coordinate handover of the body when another user occupies it. A user can commingle, or combine, their subjective reality with the reality experienced by their proxxi. For Atopians, a proxxi is a direct stand-in for its user, accorded the same respect and identity as the user themselves. Under the pssi protocols, users can only be assigned one proxxi, but they often create multiple sub-proxxi to attend several events at once. Proxxi are also the entities responsible for creating splinters, which are parts of the proxxi that are splintered off to attend or review events or appointments. This becomes a cultural convention—sending a proxxi as a full stand-in for a person for an important event, but sending only a splinter means the event's less important. The full attention of a person is termed the "primary subjective," and it is rare that a person's primary subjective would be in only one place at one time, even more rarely within their own body.

PSOMBIE

A psombie is when a human's body is occupied by a machine intelligence that has nothing to do with the person (i.e., their body is not left in the control of their proxxi or even a splinter, and they have no subjective sensory stream coming from their body that they can tap into), often when a person leases or lends their body to perform work when they don't need it—or in the event they are incarcerated for crimes, their minds will be disconnected from their bodies and imprisoned while their bodies are used to help in farming or cleaning during the sentence period. On Atopia, psombies occupy and run the vertical farming complexes as well as clean the properties.

PSSI

(This term is purposely uncapitalized because it is so commonly used)—an acronym for "poly-synthetic sensory interface." This is a platform of technologies that enables an absolutely perfect synthetic reality, a perfect sensory reconstruction of sight, sound, touch, smell, taste, plus a range of twenty-plus other senses. For example, the sense of touch by itself is made up of five senses—tactile, kinesthetic (the position and motion of limbs), sense of temperature, sense of skin being penetrated, and the proprioceptive sense of things being a part of our bodies.

The pssi-technology platform accomplishes this by intercepting and transducing afferent (from sense organs to brain) and efferent (from brain to glands and muscle) nerve signals using smarticles embedded in the body, turning the mind into a "brain in a box" that can either be presented wholly synthetic reality or a mix of reality and augmented reality. Critical in this technology platform is the ability, when pssi is installed in the nervous system of a host, to control the motor functions of the body, enabling a proxxi to control and protect the body of the user while the user is in synthetic space and/or protect the body in the event of any danger whatsoever.

Pssi enables the user to directly plug his or her mind into the informational flow of the multiverse, filtered and aided by their proxxi. It also enables the user to create phantoms and to remap their sensory system—for instance, to remap their skin to the surface of the water when surfing, or to trigger the hair in their back to stock trades so they can "feel" the stock market.

PSSI-KID

The first generation of children born on Atopia who grew up with the pssi-stimulus embedded in their nervous systems from birth. They were a part of the final clinic-trials phase of pssi as a medical device. Cognix Corporation carried out these trials on Atopia as they wouldn't have been able to receive approval for this, and many other trials, in any other jurisdiction. Pssi-kids grew up seeing very little difference between this world and purely synthetic worlds.

SLINGSHOT

An off-center rotating platform weapon that can sling thousands of pellets a second, at speeds of up to several miles per second, at incoming targets—sort of like a souped-up Gatling gun/rail gun combination. This is based on real research—imagine dropping a ball bearing into an empty beer can, and then holding the can at its base and wobbling the can around in concentric off-center rotations. The ball bearing would rapidly accelerate around the circumference of the inside of the can at high speed for very little motion or effort on your part. That's the idea, but on a much larger scale. Atopia uses batteries of slingshot, as well as a mass driver cannon (that doubles as a passenger transport) and a range of drones and other weapons systems to defend its physical assets.

SMARTICLE

These "smart particles" are the physical basis of the pssi-technology platform, nanoscale devices (about the size of a virus) that enter into and suffuse through the body of a host, automatically latching themselves along the axons of nerve cells. They derive their power from the heat of the body. Once in place, they create a sensor-communication-transduction network within the neural systems of the host, communicating and modifying nerve signals in real time. A user can typically install a smarticle network within his or her body by simply drinking a glass of water containing trillions of the invisible-to-the-eye devices. They are so small they can also float in the air, buffeted and held aloft by Brownian motion of air—on Atopia, the entire environment, air, water, etc., is infused with smarticles.

SPLINTERS

Synthetic intelligence meta-cognition constructs, which are like simulated versions of "you" (packed with as much of a user's memories and cognitive models as needed) that are sent out to investigate something or monitor an event. These splinters report back to the user in highly compressed user-specific sensory and memetic constructs understandable only to the user who owns the splinter. Imagine your best friend winking at you when someone enters a party—based on your unique shared memories and knowledge of each other, that wink, which contains only a single bit of information, forms the basis for a huge amount of conveyed information. A splinter is like this best friend, a shared-memory version of you whom you can send out and communicate with.

SYNTHETIC REALITY

An older term for virtual reality that actually takes the concept further. Rather than being virtually there, a synthetic reality can be actually and completely there, with full physical sensation, yet created wholly within an intangible environment—it could be thought of as virtual reality 2.0. Importantly, it does not need to totally replace reality, but can often be used to create an augmented reality or seamless bridges from reality to augmented reality to wholly virtual reality—the term encompasses all these modes.

Acknowledgments

I'd like to thank my beta readers (I'm sorry if I don't have all your surnames!) Dennis, Adi Sagi, Alan Shearer, Alison Hidge, Ann Christy, Justin Killam, Antoinette, Ashley, Austin McConnell, Stephen, Alex Henriksson, Bill Derb, Bill Mather, Amber, Bruce Keener, Pamela Deering, Lance Barnett, Craig Haseler, Chris Wojdak, Chrissie, Cody Parks, Dave Edmonds, Dan Norko, Esther Fraser, Scott, Alistair Gellan, Haydn Virtue, Dan, Jae Lee, Jennifer, Jon, Josh Brandoff, Joy Lu, Julie Schmidt, Allan Tierning, Ken Zufall, Lowell, Laura, Tationna Lowe, Fern Marburg, Michel, Marcus Brito, Meg Born, Chee, Olesea, Patty Gee, Phil Grave, Portia Gillespie, Justin, Rachel Wills, Loretta, Rob Linx, Rob, Sara Dieros, Josh Saliba, Shabnam Perry, Steve Siracusan, Adam, Sheila Conners, Aaron Smith, Lori Travers, Clayton, Josh, Tomas Classon, and Tom Power.

About the Author

Photo © 2013 Matthew Mather

After earning a degree in electrical engineering, Matthew Mather started his professional career at the McGill Center for Intelligent Machines. He went on to found one of the world's first tactile-feedback companies, which became the world leader in its field, as well as creating an award-winning brain-training video game. In between, he's worked on a variety of start-ups, from computational nanotechnology, electronic health records, and weather prediction systems to genomics and social-intelligence research. In 2009, the original inspiration for his technology career—reading the great masters of science fiction—set him on a new path. The result was the bestselling Atopia series, including *The Atopia Chronicles*, *The Dystopia Chronicles*, and *The Utopia Chronicles*. He is also the author of the Nomad novels, *Nomad* and *Sanctuary*, as well as *Darknet* and *CyberStorm*, the latter soon to be a major motion picture from 20th Century Fox. He divides his time between Montreal, Canada, and Charlotte, North Carolina.